Thank you
for your interest ~~

Enjoy the
reading!

Kati Fabian

EAGLES
OVER BERLIN

Novel by
Kati Fabian

Edited by Jim Woods

Photographs courtesy of
National Museum of U.S. Air Force
U.S. Air Force in Europe
Vidicom TV, Germany

FIRST NORTH AMERICAN PAPERBACK EDITION IN ENGLISH

ISBN 1-4116-2722-9
LCCN 2005924572

This story is dedicated to the ordinary men and women who realized the most important American victory of the Cold War known under the name "The Blockade of Berlin."

IN MEMORIAM OF THOSE WHO SACRIFICED THEIR LIVES

J. Anderson	R. H. Boyd	G. S. Burns
A. J. Burton	E. E. Carroll	M. E. Casey
H. R. Crites, Jr.	W. Cusack	J. M. Devolentine
E. C. Diltz	I. R. Donaldson	F. Dowling
W. Dühring	A. Dunsire	P. J. Edwards
E. S. Erickson	H. Fiedler	R. J. Freight
R. R. Gibbs	L. E. H. Gilbert	C. Golding
P. J. Griffin	L. E. Grout	G. Haan
C. v. Hagen	W. F. Hargis	R. M. W. Heath
H. F. Heinig	W. R. Howard	G. Kell
C. H. King	C. B. Ladd	D. J. Leemon
W. R. D. Lewis	P. A. Lough	W. T. Lucas
R. C. v. Luehrte	R. C. Marks	H. T. Newman
E. O'Neil	J. T. Orms	W. G. Page
H. Patterson	A. Penny	B. E. Phelps
C. L. Putman	M. J. Quinn	W. A. Rathgeber
K. A. Reeves	D. W. Robertson	K. Schlinsog
H. Schwarz	K. A. Seaborne	J. P. L. Sharp
G. B. Smith	R. C. Stephens	R. E. Stone
R. W. Stuber	T. Supernatt	C. Taylor
N. H. Thies	H. W. Thomson	J. Toal
S. M. L. Towersey	F. I. Trevona	C. W. Utting
J. A. Vaughn	B. J. Watkins	E. W. Watson
R. P. Weaver	L. C. Wells	L. A. Wheaton, Jr.
J. G. Wilkins	L. V. Williams	R. Winter
K. G. Wood	R. M. Wurgel	

AUTHOR'S NOTE

1945 –2005

Sixty years have passed since the end of World War II. A new generation has grown up and the sufferings of the war and its aftermath are only the subjects of action movies. Nevertheless, the world as we know it today was born in those days, in the middle of controversy.

In 1945, Europe was in ruins. Hunger, misery, and economic disaster ravaged the continent. Based on human desperation, Communism progressed. Tyranny and dictatorship changed color from Nazi black to Soviet red. The Americans understood the necessity to put in place a vast economic recovery program. The American taxpayers spent $16.5 Billion, representing 70 Billion of today's dollars, in economic revival of Western European countries, to stop Soviet expansionism. Without the Americans, the map of Europe would be different today.

The crisis and conflict arrived only three years after the end of World War II. In June 1948, the Soviet Army blocked West Berlin, essentially taking hostage two and half million inhabitants. They were certain the allied powers would abandon the city, opening the road for the Soviet Union to exploit Germany and all of Europe. For almost a year, the planes of the U.S. Air Force and the British RAF, like an army of majestic eagles, kept blockaded Berlin alive through the air. Every minute, a plane landed in Berlin transporting fuel, milk, coal, potatoes, instruments, wine, asphalt, pickup trucks, clothes, and all supplies necessary for the survival of the city.

The Americans arrived in Berlin as enemies in 1945. Three years later, they became friends and allies, the guardian of the freedom and the hope of two and half million Berliners. In face of the allies' tenacity and determination, the Soviets lifted the blockade in May 1949. In the heart of the Soviet sphere, an island of democracy and freedom, West Berlin, remained unvanquished.

It remained bright and appealing until the day when the fundamental principle of mankind could spread out to an entire region. In November 1989, the Berlin Wall came down and the Communist dictatorship collapsed. Without the heroism of American and British pilots and airmen, without the determination of two and half million Berliners forty years earlier, that day would never have come about.

In the frame of the thrilling love story between John Carpenter, American pilot and Esther Kohlberg, survivor of the death camp Treblinka, we follow the events of the Airlift and the everyday life of the Berliners with the exactitude of a documentary. My objective was to bring this period to the ordinary people on the street in the form of a fiction novel more readable and accessible to people than a political analysis.

Today, we face another, even more terrible enemy — terrorism. We have to draw an example from the lessons of the past. In the aftermath of World War II, the Allied Powers were able to create a strong unity. In December 1948, West Berliners without democratic experience, torn between monarchy and dictatorship, were able to choose democracy in free elections. I write these words on January 30, 2005. Today, the people of Iraq also choose democracy. Once again, a country of tribal rivalries and dark terror for decades engaged itself to democratic transformation in spite of bloody terror.

History shows us that wherever the Americans have arrived, democracy, freedom, civil rights and progress flourished in their footsteps. These are the basic principles of mankind! I hope this book will help to create a new alliance by highlighting our common values.

CONTENTS

PART I, POSTCARDS FROM THE PAST

PART II, IN THE EAGLES' NEST

PART III, BERLIN IN THOSE DAYS

PART IV, LIFE IN THE DARKNESS

PART V, MORE POSTCARDS FROM THE PAST

PART I.

POSTCARDS FROM THE PAST

Chapter 1
Washington, D.C., 1989

The long black Mercedes with darkened windows and Diplomatic Service license plates stopped at the Control Gate and, after the security check, continued slowly to the main building of the Pentagon. In the back seat, the officer in uniform arranged his tie and smoothed his jacket. He was excited. The meeting was important and he wanted to be at his best. He moved the attaché case to his knees and posed his hands around it as if protecting something.

He knew the Pentagon well. He had worked here for five years before his promotion to liaison officer for East European socialist countries. The transformation of these countries was fast. Nobody thought some years ago that an exit would be possible from these totalitarian regimes. People are gathering and their voices are claiming freedom. An air of change is on the horizon. *Will it happen in reality? Will all these disorganized and spontaneous movements of all these people have a successful conclusion? What a lucky man I am,* he thought. *Being in this service in 1989 is the chance of a lifetime.*

He traversed the main hall and waited for the elevator. He needed to concentrate for the forthcoming meeting. He felt his heart beating fast. The Colonel's secretary, Nancy, welcomed him with a nice smile.

"Hello Lieutenant! Did you have a good trip? Please, wait a second. The Colonel is on the phone."

Two other persons entered the office: another officer, Major Jim Spencer, and a civilian. Peter did not know him.

The Colonel appeared on the doorstep. "Good morning, Gentlemen! The General called me. Let's go together to the meeting room right away."

The four men crossed the hallway with firm steps, the Colonel first, the two officers behind him and the civilian completed the group. He had a little smile on the face. *Oh, these military types... always the same... They are not able to bypass the discipline and formalities!*

General Howell was waiting in the meeting room. He touched a big cigar in the interior pocket of his vest. He felt he would give anything to take it out and light it. That was not possible, not yet. He greeted the arriving four men and everyone took a seat around the big, oak meeting table, the main furniture of the room.

"Gentlemen, you of the military know each other, but let me introduce Mister Howard Hendricks, international lawyer, advisor on foreign affairs and specialist in the questions of Eastern Europe and the Soviet Union. He reports to the Senate and directly to the President. He is here in an advisory capacity. Mister Hendricks, let me introduce you to Lieutenant Peter Slauter, liaison officer charged to reunite all the necessary information on Eastern Europe, and to Major Jim Spencer, charged to maintain steady liaison with the CIA. You already know Colonel Richard Austin. Peter, it is up to you. What is the situation in Eastern Europe?"

"The situation is confused. Forces of the progress are in motion, but facing internal resistance from the conservative side of the political hierarchy. The question is, in the event of a conservative takeover of the situation, would military intervention be possible, and in that event, what action would we undertake in response."

Peter felt the attention turned toward him and he relaxed.

"During the last meeting in December 1988, Gorbachev met George Bush and outgoing President Ronald Reagan, and they declared their decision to end the Cold War. Now, the people of Hungary, Poland and Czechoslovakia want to have the right to choose their own futures. In the last forty years, the Soviet Union intervened in the same situation. In 1953, Soviet forces defeated the workers' uprising in Berlin. In 1956, the Soviet tanks ended the Hungarian revolution in a bloodbath. The Soviet Union used the context of the Warsaw Pact organization to crush the Spring of Prague in 1968. The introduction of martial law alone stopped the Soviet tanks invading Poland in 1981."

"What are the actual Soviet forces in place in Eastern Europe?" asked Colonel Richard Austin.

Peter took out some documents from his suitcase and went to the projector. A map of Europe appeared on the screen showing the Soviet Forces stationed in the region. Peter continued his presentation.

"Now, in 1989, the Soviet forces consist of eighty-five thousand troops in Czechoslovakia, sixty-five thousand in Hungary, fifty-eight thousand in Poland, and three hundred and eighty-eight thousand troops in East Germany. The equipment in men and material has always been on wartime level."

"Wait a second. You're driving me crazy, Lieutenant," Mister Hendricks spoke up, nervously. "You were right to mention the decision to end the Cold War. You also know that Mister Gorbachev and the Soviet Union proposed a reduction of the armed forces in the region. The first reduction will take place this summer in Hungary. Your presentation over-dramatizes the problem!"

"Not at all, Mister Hendricks!" Major Jim Spencer said seriously. "The armed forces are executing orders. The question is who is in the position to give orders. You're right; it is improbable that Mister Gorbachev would give an order for military intervention."

"We all know, however," continued the Major, "that Mister Gorbachev's program of political and economic reform is facing strong opposition from obscure political forces. We also know that the most consistent resistance is coming from his military. The Soviet military strategy remains a 'science of victory' in armed conflict. In other words, their aim was and still is today the complete defeat of the adversary. They are mistrustful of political solutions. If a conservative military were in the position of giving orders, the possibility of an armed intervention is more than improbable."

Hendricks leaned back in his seat. The Major sealed the argument in concrete. Peter took over his presentation.

"It is clear that the Soviet leaders are convinced that these countries will choose socialism with a human face and will keep up ties of friendship with the Soviet Union. What would happen if

3

non-Communists came to power? Would the Soviet Union, in fact, stand aside? How will the present communist leaders react when they feel the power slipping from their hands?"

Peter intended to give a short analysis by countries.

"Hungary, Poland and Czechoslovakia are about to introduce a multi-party system, and to talk about free elections. The Warsaw Pact is changing face also. Founded as a response to NATO, the Soviet Union used the military organization to keep its Eastern European allies under its political and military control, allowing them only 'limited' sovereignty. They are sovereign as long as they do not damage the interests of the socialist community.

"In recent years, disputes have arisen between member states, wanting to conduct their defense politics in an independent way. The atmosphere on the Warsaw Pact meetings became favorable to the clash between the forces of progress and conservatism."

Jim Spencer nodded with full comprehension and added, "We have clear information about a conspiracy of traditional communist leaders to use military forces to regain control on the situation. They are trying to talk Gorbachev and other Soviet leaders into military intervention against Poland and Hungary at this moment."

"That is the second dangerous point of the situation," continued Peter. "In the moment of crisis and in a strongly endangered situation, the traditional leaders would be tempted and able to have independent control on the military forces."

Hendricks felt uneasy and upset at the same time. The arguments he heard were indisputable and he was already aware of the major part of them. The military escalation though, came across as a minor point in the political structure of the region, and he did not consider it. He was convinced that for the first time, a revolution would succeed without bloodshed. He felt the urgency to cool down the officers.

"Gentlemen, according to the American position, we want to assist Gorbachev and the reformers in the region. President Bush wants to hold out the promise of an alternative future by convincing the American business community to seriously invest in the region.

"The President forecasts a trip to the East European countries. We will, moreover," continued Hendricks, "take some popular steps for these people. After the re-establishment of the democracy, we will hand over the crown of Saint Stephen to the Hungarian people. We also will hand over to the Czechoslovakian people their Declaration of Independence. The United States preserved these national artifacts. Their delivery to the peoples to whom they belong will boost the overall enthusiasm in favor of freedom and democracy. Your military approach suggests the contrary, and I cannot agree with that."

Colonel Austin smiled. The military approach always appeared excessive to civilians.

"Mister Hendricks, we do not forecast a military escalation. The Soviets always had plans for a conventional, rapid war destroying the European free forces before the Americans could intervene. We have to be ready for the improbable situation. You would be the first to criticize us in the contrary."

Hendricks acquiesced. General Howell took a deep breath. They had spoken enough about theory. They needed to be practical. *We are military, you bet!* He took over direction of the meeting.

"We need first-hand information, and we must send an observer to the front lines, preparing for that extreme case," commented the General.

"You are crazy!" Hendricks was nervous. He leaned backwards in his seat and began to tap his finger on the table. "It would be unreasonable to send a military officer from the Pentagon to the center of all this action! Allowing an American officer to circulate in the region will generate more fears to the KGB and push the Soviet conservatives toward action. We have already the CIA on the site, why another military observer?"

"We need to know more," intervened Colonel Austin. "As military intelligence, we have to prepare our Central Command by drawing up an action plan for rapid implementation if necessary."

General Howell was unable to bear the tension any longer. Jumping to his feet, he paced back and forth in the room. He took the cigar out of his pocket and put it in his mouth.

"General, smoking is forbidden in this facility."

"Damned! I know! I will not light it, but I have to think!"

"If you want an observer, send a civilian."

"We are a military organization; a civilian will never understand our priorities."

"It is not true, General. I am not military; I am able, though, to understand your priorities. Do not forget, in the last step, the civilian government commands you. Please, do not belittle me as a civilian."

"And you, do not belittle the military organization!"

Silence ruled for a moment. Hendricks contemplated his nails, Peter Slauter buried himself deep in his file, Jim Spencer leaned back in his seat, crossing his hands behind his head, and Richard Austin's eyes followed the General's movements.

"Send a veteran," suggested Hendricks.

"What?"

"Yes. Send a veteran. He's a civilian, but is a military also. That is a good marriage."

"What would I do with a veteran of the Vietnam War in Eastern Europe?"

"Take one from World War II! There are still former military men alive from that era. Some are still active. A man with life experience would be the best for that mission. He will be able to consider human aspects and feelings in addition to simple observation of facts."

General Howell sat back and punched in a number on the phone. "Who's in charge of our veteran organizations? No, I need someone able to look into the files and make some selections. Yes, he's good. Is he here now? ... Good. Ask him to join us in the meeting room."

They were waiting in silence, once again everyone going back to his thoughts.

Sergeant James Krosensky entered the room.

"Sergeant, I want you to go over the personnel files of our veteran organizations from World War II and set up a list of persons who are still active, in good physical shape, and could be ready for a mission in Eastern Europe."

"Sergeant," intervened Howard Hendricks, "look for someone who was in Europe at the end of the War, perhaps in Germany. This would narrow your search."

Sergeant Krosensky turned his eyes momentarily, and after the General nodded, said, "Yes, Sir!"

"Sergeant, how much time you need for this?"

"We have the list in a database. I will run a query. I can come back with some names in a half an hour."

"Could you do that from here?" The General pointed to the desktop computer on the side table.

"Yes, of course!"

Krosensky took his place in front of the computer while the others waited in silence. He exchanged a nod of friendship with Peter Slauter who came closer to the computer, interested.

"I have here three men participating actively in veteran organizations over the past five years. One man is a seventy-five year old from Arkansas. He was in Patton's division. Another is a sixty-eight year old from Texas, a former pilot. The third one is from Michigan, a seventy-two year old who was in the Navy."

"Take the youngest one, this pilot. Who is he?" asked Hendricks.

"John Carpenter, Texas, San Antonio. He received the military cross for his action in combat and was in Germany until 1950. He was also on a mission in Berlin. I mean West Berlin."

"That's good!" The General was satisfied. The profile of this former pilot was what they were looking for. This Hendricks had a good idea.

"Lieutenant Slauter! Coordinate with Krosensky, and go over the personnel file. Fly to Texas to persuade this Carpenter to accept the mission. I need to see him in my office in three days. Gentlemen! Thank you for your participation."

Chapter 2
The Texan Pilot

A beautiful sunset marked the early summer evening. Under a chestnut tree, John Carpenter sipped ice-cold lemonade. He placed his tennis racquet next to him and was thinking about this afternoon's tennis match. He managed to win once again and it was a good feeling.

After his homecoming from the war, he founded a small airline company that specialized in freight transport. He adored flying and still piloted planes sometimes. His company began with a C-54, a surplus military airplane that he knew well from Germany. The plane was a masterpiece of aviation, a non-destructible, ever flying, "Skymaster". The company still had one. Now and then, he and his pilot friends still took the old machine out for a tour above the Rio Grande.

He watched the ranch. Texas has an air of magic. The vast land stretched out in the unknown and beyond the horizon, the wilderness was still waiting. After many years of civilization, the landscape remained the same untouched beauty. He has his roots in that earth, under that sun; he felt linked to that chestnut tree and to that woman.

"John! Jessica is on the line! Come on!"

Oh, my daughter. He placed the glass on the table and entered the house.

Veronica gave him the phone, left him alone, and went into the kitchen. She prepared a small dinner for both of them. Through the open door, she watched her husband's tall figure. She remembered the young officer coming back from Germany after they had met at a ball in Houston. His demeanor was sad, but once released, his smile shined. The past had marked him. His reserve and his timidity aroused her maternal instincts. She found in him a companion, a friend, a lover, and a family man. She felt privileged having him on her side.

The sudden noise of a car broke the serenity of the sunset. The car stopped before the house and a young officer walked up to the doorstep.

"Hello. Mrs. Carpenter?"

"Yes. Hello…"

"I'm Lieutenant Peter Slauter from Washington. May I speak with your husband?"

"Yes, he is here," she said, with a trembling voice. *What's going on? John is no longer involved in the military! He left the army years ago and a veteran's meeting would not call for an officer to come from Washington to Texas.* She was alarmed.

In the living room, John greeted the young officer with the same mistrust as his wife had, but also he felt some excitement in his heart. "Please sit down."

The living room was comfortable and welcoming. Amongst the paintings and decoration, Peter saw the photo of an old airplane with a young soldier and he recognized John Carpenter. He noticed an old-fashioned wooden tennis racquet on the wall, an evident souvenir of past glory. *This Carpenter is hanging on to memories. The old man does not seem old. He still plays tennis. I saw another tennis racquet as I entered. He looks younger than his age,* Peter thought.

"Mister Carpenter. I'm here to propose to you the mission of observer in Eastern Europe. As you are aware, perhaps through some television reports, things are moving fast there. The Central Command needs an observer in place. Preferring a veteran civilian for that job, we propose this mission to you."

John was amazed, but felt honored at the same time. Forgotten memories came to the surface at once. Eastern Europe and Germany… That was long ago! He took an old watch out of his pocket, distraught, and played with it nervously.

"I am no longer in service, and also, I was not involved in the question of intelligence. I was a simple pilot."

"Not so simple, Mister Carpenter. I saw your personnel file; you were an excellent pilot."

"Yes, there were several others, though. I had the chance to survive. Many of my friends sacrificed their lives over Europe, and in particular, over Germany."

"You said it, Mister Carpenter. In your time, we destroyed fascist Germany. After the War with the Marshall Plan, we reconstructed West Germany, but we left East Germany to the Soviets. Now, all people there want to vacate that communist regime."

"Yes, we heard about these movements on television."

"We are not able to foresee the Soviet reaction. People are in motion and repeating one word, 'freedom.'"

"What would be my role as this 'observer?'"

"You will inform us on the general situation. Our military advisors will do the rest."

Peter spoke convincingly, and hoped for an immediate decision. He hoped to transmit to John Carpenter his passion.

"Mister Slauter, I mean Lieutenant Slauter, would you have dinner with us? We were ready to sit down at the table." Veronica broke up the discussion and this unnerved Peter. He hoped that he had succeeded in his persuasive tasks and he was afraid to begin once again.

"Yes, thank you, if I do not disturb..."

"No, not at all. We will have dinner under the chestnut tree in the garden."

They went all together to the table. Veronica returned to the kitchen to get the mashed potatoes and John lit the barbecue. It will be a traditional Texan dinner — T-bone steak, mashed potatoes and salad.

Following dinner, at the bar, pouring scotch for the men and cherry liquor for Veronica, John's attention fell on the photos on the fireplace. He went over to them and took one particular photo in his hand. The photo was an old one, yellow from age. In the photo was a young pilot in uniform and a young girl. Both were smiling and an air of happiness shone through the photo. John stared to his own young face in the photo and was in deep thought; he did not hear his wife returning to the living room.

Veronica knew the photo and her heart trembled. She had always been jealous of that girl and felt that memories were coming back, and she did not like it.

"John, we are waiting."

"Oh, yes." John replaced the photograph on the fireplace. "I was just thinking."

"Oh John, after so many years, are you still in love with her?"

John laughed. "No, Veronica. You know I love you. Those were my young years and that is a woman I loved. You know the whole story. My young years are gone, but the memories are still here. This young officer has come with the proposal to go back to the places I have already lived. I am thinking about it."

Veronica approached him and put her arms around his neck. "I love you, John. Whatever you decide, I will agree to."

They stood there in each other's arms for a moment without saying anything.

Peter was ready to leave and as he called for the car, John told him, "Lieutenant, I accept this mission."

Two weeks later, John took his seat on a Boeing 767 en route to West Berlin. He had a fluttery feeling in his stomach. This flight had a special aura. He leaned back in the seat. The engines revved, and he felt the movement of takeoff. The plane reached a high altitude and the memories came back of those days when he was in the pilot's seat and the undiscovered mysteries of life were still waiting for him.

PART II.

IN THE EAGLES' NEST

Chapter 3
Germany, 1945

The noise of the engine was familiar to the young pilot. In these past years, this noise was his life. After special training, he received his orders to the European Theatre of Operations and participated in many missions. In the heart of the action, when danger was imminent, he was never scared; he had no time for it. Enemy fighters coming from everywhere — Shouting in his ears — The planes of his friends in flames — No, he had no time for fear. After landing, when he realized that close friends were lost in the fighting, he had cramps in his stomach. Later, when the war was over, flying became a joy without limit.

He moved into position for landing and concentrated on the approach. He was skilled with the instruments and landed, as usual, with perfect style.

The other planes of the squadron landed also. The young pilots were happy to find each other on the ground. Their youthful joy, their healthy laughter and their impetuous temperament contrasted to the dark days of war.

"Hey, John! Let's have a beer." Pete always organized some meetings or social events. The squadron went together and these were always good times.

The base in Rhein-Main had a well maintained bar. They were not able to go anywhere from the base. Germany was in ruins. Allied bombardments had destroyed whole towns; industrial regions ceased to exist. Sometimes the pilots escaped to Wiesbaden, the next airfield or went to Frankfurt. That made him sad. Frankfurt was a field of desolation.

He always had a strange feeling looking at these ruins. The bombs destroyed the facades; showing the wallpaper-covered or painted walls of living rooms and bedrooms, where people lived before. The walls told a long story about the intimate life of the occupants. Loneliness, sorrow, and despair filled his heart. He felt embarrassed for this deep insight into the naked intimacy of unknown people. The children playing between these ruins made the situation even more absurd.

Money had no value. They were able to have everything with cigarettes, young women, especially. These women were mothers, daughters, and sisters. They provided the means of survival for aged parents, hungry children, and crippled brothers. Yes, cigarettes were everything. The black market was flourishing between the different areas of the country.

The allies cut Germany into different occupational zones, even Berlin had four sectors: American, British, French, and Soviet. John wondered, how it would function. Once, they had several days' leave and wanted to drive to Berlin, but they were not able to cross the Soviet zone. Too many controls, too much waiting; they lost patience. These Soviets always had excuses for anything.

He remembered the euphoric first days of victory. When the two fronts met at the River Elbe, Soviet soldiers came over to greet the Americans and the British. In the sky, the fighters saluted each other and a feeling of comradeship spread out in the air. Once, he had the chance to meet Soviet fighter pilots.

John recognized Aleksey Marasyev, legendary Soviet pilot, who had mastered both aircraft and artificial legs. In 1942, he was shot down by the Luftwaffe, badly injuring both legs. It took nineteen days to crawl back to Russian lines. When the partisans found him, the doctors had to amputate both legs because of gangrene. John respected Marasyev. The Russians merited a better life than what the communists were able to offer them.

The euphoria of the friendship did not last for long. Soon, the political commissars stopped any communication between the armies. They instituted the controls and the harassment began. The future was uncertain.

The pilots arrived in the cantina. Life took over the war and they were laughing and joking once again without fear of tomorrow.

Chapter 4
Zhukov 's Satisfaction

Marshal Zhukov leaned back in his seat in Soviet Military Headquarters. He represented the Soviet Union at the signing of the German surrender, and had an overwhelming international reputation. He was the most talented and, for sure, the most successful military leader of the Soviet Union. One minute ago, his adjutant gave him a note from the American and British Military Commanders. He had to make a decision.

He was nineteen years old when he entered the Russian imperial Army in 1914, and first studied strategy in Germany under General von Seeckt. The father of the Red Army, Leon Trotsky took him over into the newly born People's Army. Trotsky trusted many officers from the Tsarist army. Zhukov never forgot that. He was a military man from the heart, and an excellent strategist.

The Marshal knew his decision had to please those in Moscow. He remembered the great purges in 1937 and 1938 when the secret police arrested and executed about thirty five thousand good men of the officer corps. Stalin made a good choice when he spared Zhukov at the time. Marshal Zhukov participated in all major battles of the Great Patriotic War from Leningrad through Moscow to Stalingrad and was a pioneer of using tanks in decisive battle. His aristocratic stature dominated the battlefield. He led the final attack on Berlin with a firm hand, commanding eight hundred-thousand men, twelve thousand cannons, three thousand six hundred tanks, and three thousand aircraft.

Now, he was at the peak of his military career and he had to give an answer to the exigencies of the allied military commanders. "The Allied Forces must obtain the unlimited right to access highways, railroads and waterways leading to the allied sectors, allowing them to maintain their troops, to exercise their function, and use the best transport available for this purpose. The establishment of clear rules for the sky is also necessary."

Marshal Zhukov smiled. *Of course, they want free access in order to maneuver in Soviet territory! Their troops are not able to survive without communications and maintenance,* he thought. He went to the window. The Red Army soldiers, used to extreme hardship, were different. They did not need communication columns to survive. He felt proud. The Russian soldiers amassed behind the tanks and as vast hordes on horseback or on foot rolled over the enemies. In their backpacks, they had dry crusts of breads and raw vegetables from the fields and villages. The horses ate straw from the roofs of houses. Westerners were not able to even imagine that. He won battles during the Civil War against the Whites with exhausted but brave cavalries. Zhukov corrected himself: the Soviet soldiers. He looked around the room to ensure he was alone and that nobody was there to observe or hear his subversive thoughts.

The Marshal remembered the unfortunate defender of Minsk, General Pavlov, well. After the defeat at Minsk, Stalin charged General Pavlov with incompetence, and ordered his execution. The people of Minsk did not have luck either. The German Army massacred the inhabitants of the town. Terrified of both Stalin and Hitler, the Soviet people had no option but to fight until they died.

Twenty-seven million Soviet civilians and soldiers did not live to see the day of the victory. Their tribute is unforgettable. The words of Lenin echoed in his head: "Whoever has Germany has Europe." Zhukov intended to not give up any inches of the obtained advantages.

The intentions of Moscow were clear. They had already begun to put local administration in place, headed by communists. The Soviet Army installed German communist leaders living in the Soviet Union to head German political life. Walter Ulbricht and Wilhelm Pieck in Berlin, and Anton Ackerman in Dresden, had already begun to select city officials. They installed Communists as heads of education and the police in each district. The Soviet Union would have their hands on the present and on the future.

His attention went back to the note on his desk. The Soviet Allied Forces were in charge of maintaining road and traffic conditions. The repair and maintenance of the destroyed roads and bridges was expensive and time consuming. This was a volatile argument. The Allied Military Commandments had no means of verifying that. He called his adjutant and ordered, firmly, "We will continue to negotiate, but we will not concede anything to them. In any case, we will sign nothing."

Marshal Zhukov felt this is the decision that would please the leader in Moscow. He already knew his presence in Berlin could be counted in days. His successor was General Sokolovsky; the two men were not on good terms. The choice of his rival made Zhukov uncertain of his future. He might be a Hero of the Soviet Union, a world-known military commander, but Stalin likely would despise his fame.

Once again, he remembered Trotsky. Total revolution... when Trotsky spoke about it, he had to escape from the Soviet Union. An agent of the Soviet Secret Service murdered him in Mexico, on Stalin's order. *And now? What we are doing now? We are doing just that: the promulgation of our revolution! Europe will be Red in some years and we will lead the Americans by their noses.* He felt extreme satisfaction after all.

Chapter 5
The Covenant

John Carpenter waited in the hangar. The squadron was going on a mission today. Winter was strong here, but today the smell of spring spread in the air. *What a beautiful day for flying!*

The pilots took their places in the fighters. The takeoff was as smooth as the flight of birds. One-hour air patrol, the regular exercise that was the order: nothing else, than the joy of flying.

All of a sudden, John noticed something strange — engine noise, but not at all familiar... *What is that?* The Soviet fighters came from nowhere. They came at high speed at the Americans, crossing their direction. They tried to avoid each other and executed some difficult maneuvers. John became nervous and fear filled his soul. They were not prepared for an encounter and everything was happening fast.

"Pete — there is one behind you, go higher, go, go, go — my God you have to gain altitude!"

It was too late; the collision was unavoidable. The two fighters went up in flames...

John had tears in his eyes and asked himself, *what happened? Is Pete dead?* Yes, he saw that. He himself was losing control of his machine. He had to concentrate and to take control of his emotions. Flight control ordered him to land at the closest American airport, Tempelhof, in Berlin.

When the ground crew took him out of the plane, John's legs were trembling, and he was crying like a child. Pete had survived the war, many air combats, and now he was dead in a peacetime collision.

The airport personnel of Tempelhof had already informed the Central Command on what happened. General Doolittle was furious. Several collisions and accidents occurred in the last days and weeks and that was the third dead pilot of the peace. He had to take action at once.

General Doolittle was one of the most famous pilots in the American Air Force. In the early 1920's, he made the first cross-country flight from Florida to California in twenty-one hours. Some years later, on demonstration flight, he executed breathtaking aerial maneuvers with his two broken ankles in casts. He earned major air trophies and international fame.

The stubborn young man became lieutenant colonel in 1942 and he planned, commanded, and executed the first aerial raid on Tokyo, intended to pay back the Japanese for Pearl Harbor. Without his overwhelming enthusiasm, the courageous enterprise would not have succeeded. This daring one-way raid electrified the world.

As Lieutenant General in the European Theatre of Operation, he decided to use all his fame and influence to settle this matter with his Soviet counterpart.

The driver of the jeep braking in front of John was in a hurry. "General Doolittle wants to see you at once. You have to report all details to him."

John tried to compose himself. He put his memories in military order. The jeep stopped in front of the Central Command building. In the hallway, General Doolittle was waiting for him.

"We are going right away to Commandant Kozhedub. You report to me on the way," the General ordered the young pilot. "What happened?"

"We were on patrol — simple, routine patrol. We thought the flight was free and the corridor was open. We did not receive any information from Flight Control. They did not know anything about Soviet air activities."

They arrived nervous, impatient and upset at the office of Commandant Kozhedub.

"The Commandant is with Air Force officers, you have to wait."

"That is even better, and I'm not waiting." General Doolittle hurried into the office; the Soviet officers were surprised. At the same time, they felt ashamed for their own excitement, which they were unable to control.

Commandant Ivan Kozhedub was the leading Allied flying ace of World War II. He had sixty-two victories. The Americans envied his title. The Soviet pilots flew in combat until they died. Commandant Kozhedub managed to survive the war because of his exceptional flying skills.

The Americans were more familiar with the other officer, Aleksandr Pokryshkin who survived the war with fifty-nine victories. He realized forty-eight of those in the fighter called "Aircobra", delivered to the Soviet Union by the United States in the Lend-Lease Agreement. Pokryshkin mastered this airplane. He was standing in front of Commandant Kozhedub, nervously agitating.

The Soviets were upset and protesting. So were the Americans. Everyone was losing their tempers. English words mixed with the Russian, they spoke all at the same time. They did not need an interpreter.

"You have to admit that we need regulation of the sky!"

"You will not make your own rules compulsory to us!"

"Why do we not set up a Control Counsel in order to work out the common rules?"

The tension lowered. They agreed to create the Berlin Air Safety Center.

"I want you to participate in that group," the General told John, when they were leaving the building. "You were the eyewitness of that accident and you must represent the pilots in that committee."

John was surprised and honored. He had the sudden feeling that he would do something for the construction of a new era and he will be more useful. It was an amazing feeling.

Three corridors, each twenty miles wide, were opened for allied aircraft, leading to the British and the American airports, allowing connection with the British, American, and French sectors of Berlin.

The aircraft had to maintain a flight level between nine-hundred and about ten-thousand feet. All flights had to signal their takeoff, landing, and destination. The Council also determined methods and instruments used to control the visibility and the follow-up of flights.

The Western representatives made it clear — the American and British Air Forces would consider any interruption of the Soviet Air Force into the corridors as an act of war.

The Berlin Air Safety Center had to ensure diplomatically the safety of allied air traffic into and out of the Western sectors of Berlin. The Allied Control Council building housed also the Berlin Air Safety Center. The Center consisted of American, British, and French military representatives along with two Soviet representatives, a controller and an interpreter.

The security of the air traffic ameliorated fast. John was fascinated. Through his interesting work in that commission he understood how many rules, instruments and human attention was necessary to conclude a successful mission.

The Allied Forces held a conference in Potsdam, near Berlin, in July 1945, with the objective of implementing the decisions reached earlier at the Yalta Conference. They did not sign any agreement regarding circulation and traffic. The unique document signed from this respect was a single covenant of air safety regularization.

Chapter 6
The Iron Curtain

The train traversed the large agricultural fields of Missouri nearing the little town, Fulton, with its usual less than ten thousand inhabitants. On that day of March 1946, the early spring began to wake up the vegetation, and beautiful green bushes were blooming along the otherwise empty roads. These roads, however, were not empty today. In long lines, many cars were nearing the Victorian downtown of Fulton. The people headed for Westminster College, a well-known establishment of the county. The flags were up in the little town, where today around forty thousand people gathered to welcome two leaders — Winston Churchill and Harry Truman.

Churchill had lost the last elections at home. He did not take the defeat kindly, although today, he was delighted to be here as a private person. He felt free to express thoughts, which haunted him for a while. A great silence ensued when he stepped up to the podium. The public did not yet know they would be witnesses to a historic event, changing the political situation of the world. Churchill spoke calmly, but with conviction.

"From Stettin in the Baltic to Trieste in the Adriatic, an iron curtain has descended across the Continent. Behind that line lie all the capitals of the ancient states of Central and Eastern Europe. Warsaw, Berlin, Prague, Vienna, Budapest, Belgrade, Bucharest and Sofia, all these famous cities and the populations around them lie in what I must call the Soviet sphere, and all are subject in one form or another, not only to Soviet influence but to a very high and, in many cases, increasing measure of control from Moscow. Whatever conclusions may be drawn from these facts — and facts they are — this is certainly not the Liberated Europe we fought to build up. Nor is it one, which contains the essentials of permanent peace. In a great number of countries, far from the Russian frontiers and throughout the world, Communist fifth columns are established and work in complete unity and absolute obedience to the directions they receive from the Communist center."

The faces of political advisors around Truman went white. This was an open attack on Stalin and the Soviet Union! The American foreign policy at that time consisted of trying to get along with the Soviet Union and allowing Churchill to pronounce these words might jeopardize the current negotiations in Europe.

Truman put on a serious face in front of his advisors, but inside, he was smiling. He had met Stalin once, at the Potsdam Conference in 1945. His first impression of the "Man of Steel" was optimistic. He thought Stalin was the man he would be able to deal with when it came to negotiations. He was soon disappointed. Stalin and the Soviets were relentless bargainers, forever pressing for every advantage.

The war left Europe devastated thus pushing the European democracies towards the left. The most ravaged land was Germany. The German people were starving and dying by the thousands. Coincidental to the reorganization of the European borders, the new local authorities expelled the German tribes living for several generations in Poland and in the Soviet Union. The Polish and Russian peoples took revenge on them for the atrocities of the Nazis. The expelled Germans, for the most part women, children and the elderly, became fugitives gathered in the Western zones, if they arrived there at all. Two million of them died along the road somewhere in Central Europe. These fugitives without any resources were in the charge of the Allied Administrations in the Western zones.

Truman had serious discussions with Churchill in the train. The British Empire was dying. The French were prisoners of their leftists and communists, who were an essential part of the resistance. Now, they wanted to have their share of political power. Italy also was trembling, with a communist party becoming the best-organized political structure in the country. The European nations were starving. Communism progresses when the people lose their hope for a better life. Truman was determined to keep their hope alive.

Harry Truman knew the man he wanted for that mission, the son of a prosperous coal businessperson in Pennsylvania who became a soldier against the will of the family. The young officer distinguished himself in World War I serving as aide-de-camp of General Pershing. After the attack on Pearl Harbor, he became responsible for the building, supplying and, in part, deploying of over eight million soldiers. The career of the General, resigned from the military in 1945, was about to take a new turn.

President Truman traversed the Oval Office to greet his Secretary of State, the newly nominated General George Marshall.

"Please, be seated," said President Truman, pointing to the big comfortable armchair in the corner of the Oval Office. "May I call you, George, General Marshall?"

"No, Mister President. General Marshall will do," answered the austere, unapproachable man. He exuded leadership and character. He arrived from his European inspection tour that included Moscow, and he wanted to see the President right away.

"Mister President, after my two hour meeting with Stalin in the Kremlin, I am convinced that the Soviets are stalling for time. They speculate that the situation in Western and Central Europe will become increasingly adverse and the consecutive popular unrest would become proportionally greater. The communists would grow in strength and maybe communist regimes would come to power in Western Europe even without the intervention of the Red Army."

"How did you find the economic situation in Europe overall?" inquired the President. "The analysis on my desk reports major problems."

"Correct. The world situation is serious. The breakdown of the business structure of Europe during the war was complete. The rehabilitation of the economic structure of the entire continent, as far as we know, will require a much longer time and greater effort than we have foreseen."

President Truman was not surprised. He awaited Marshall's assessment. "General, I have the feeling we understand each other. The remedy of the situation remains in the restoration of confidence. The European people have to believe in the economic future of their own countries and of Europe as a whole."

"The truth is," added General Marshall, "that the European countries must have substantial additional help from America or they will face economic, social and political deterioration of a grave character."

"I understood that well, General," replied Truman. "For that reason, I was looking for somebody to lead this battle for the return of normal economic health in the world. Without the economic health, there would be no political stability and assured peace. We have to direct our policy against hunger, poverty, desperation, and chaos."

George Marshall had a serious expression on his face. "I must underline, Mister President, the American taxpayer will have difficulty to comprehend these mass facts presented by the medias. The people of this country are distant from the troubled areas of the earth and it will perhaps be hard for them as taxpayers to understand the necessity of these actions and their costs to the American people."

"General, political passion and prejudice should have no part in that matter." Truman spoke with enthusiasm. He felt charged with a mission. "I am confident that our people will face up to the vast responsibility, which history has without a doubt placed upon our country."

When General Marshall left the Oval Office, President Truman was sure he had chosen the right man. *I am convinced he is the great one of the age... the Architect of Peace,* thought President Harry Truman.

The vastest Economic Recovery Program, named for George Marshall also included a specific plan regarding Germany. Truman and Marshall realized that the postwar restoration of Europe involved the restoration of Germany. Without the revival of Germany, there would be no revival in Europe. The reorganization of Germany had to include the implementation of a political structure with German government, free enterprise, free trade and the introduction of a new currency. It would be the first time in history that the victors rebuilt the vanquished.

It was also clear to the two men that the Soviet Union, and Stalin personally, would not agree with these dispositions. They will maneuver to block the recovery of other countries thus seeking to perpetuate human misery in order to profit from it for political purposes.

The supreme conflict was still to come.

Chapter 7
Sweet Home

After the amazing work in the Berlin Air Safety Center, John Carpenter returned to the base, to his usual activities. This evening, he went with his fellow pilots from the squadron to a locale in Frankfurt where military personal and officers came together.

This night, as usual, they were sitting at a table, when three girls stepped in. John already knew two of them, but he saw the third one for the first time. She was a remarkable young person. Her skin was almost transparent, fine and white, and she was tall and slender. Her blonde hair shimmered with a slight red tint. Her large green eyes amazed him the most. *What a smile she has,* he thought.

"Hi, I'm John Carpenter."

"Hello, John. Esther Kohlberg," and now the smile changed into a good laugh. She had a singing, agreeable accent.

When she took off her blazer he saw the tattoo number in her forearm. *Oh, that is it! She is a Jew, a survivor!* John learned with horror the atrocities committed by the Nazis in the death camps. *How is she able to be as bright, as optimistic? The extreme sufferings she had to endure in the camp had not curbed her spirit. She must have a strong personality.*

"You speak English well."

"We learned in the family from books as resistance to the Soviet regime. It was a sign of freedom. I am from the Soviet Union, you know. We did not have freedom and there is still no freedom. My grandfather had the conviction that the resistance of the mind is more important than physical opposition. As always, he was right. I never spoke English before arriving to the American sector."

"You made a long journey."

"Oh yes, I did…"

For a moment, Esther was going back to her memories. She was twenty, but had gone through enough for two lifetimes. She saw the face of her grandfather; a Rabin native to Halle in Germany, who came to the Yeshiva, married her grandmother and stayed with her in the neighborhood of Lvov.

The whereabouts of that frontier land was uncertain for centuries. Poland, Russia, and even the Habsburg Monarchy annexed the territory. Within the bounds imposed on them, the Jewish culture flourished. Although enjoying royal protection and communal autonomy, the Jewish communities had to face severe anti-Semitism. Forbidden to own land, the Jews served as estate managers and intermediaries between nobility and peasants, often collecting taxes for the nobles, controlling the sale of salt and fish, ran the grain mills, and owned local village taverns. As a result, besides disliking them as foreigners and non-Christians, the peasants held Jews responsible for their own oppressed and miserable lives. The sovereignty changed, but all governments were alike, maintaining and exploiting these resentments, and the Jews became victims of pogroms, persecutions, and massacres.

Esther remembered grandfather's radiant face in the first years of the Soviet state. Many Jews supported the creation of the new, "non-national" state, hoping it would tolerate Jews. The educated Jews found their way into Soviet cultural and economic life, in particular higher education and scientific institutions. Many Jews occupied important positions in the party leadership. This euphoria did not last long.

The Jewish leaders became the first victims in the great purges of Stalin in the early 1930s. Stalin tortured and executed his closest Jewish partners, Zinoviev, Kamenev, and Litvinov. They all perished in the purges. When they persecuted even the Jewish born Trotsky, the disillusion of grandfather was complete. He came home with the English book and they began their passive resistance to the Soviet regime that forbade not only speaking, but also thinking.

When the German Army arrived in Ukraine, they annihilated the Jews. Many local people helped the Nazis. At first, Esther thought herself to be lucky, being put in the concentration camp of Treblinka.

That would save her from the blind cruelty in the village. She soon understood how wrong she was. Grandfather wanted everyone in the family to speak correct German as a tie to his origins. He did not know that this knowledge would save his granddaughter's life. She was fifteen and decided to survive the surrounding everyday horrors. The Soviet Army liberated the camp, but that did not mean freedom for her. The Soviet regime rejected the Jews.

Salvation came from the Americans when officers were looking for facts and witnesses for the Nuremberg Process. She took a deep breath and for the first time in her life, she spoke some English words. It was incomprehensible to the American officers, but they understood she would be able to help them. The Americans transferred her to Nuremberg, into the American sector. The Soviets wanted to cooperate and authorized the temporary transfer. She never turned back. Now, a free life awaited her.

Esther examined the young American officer. He was tall with black eyes and brown hair, and had a tender smile. Pilots have an outgoing personality. She liked at the first instant this person who was looking at her with certain timidity.

Next day, when John Carpenter was returning to the Rhein-Main Air Base by bus, he was amazed to see Esther Kohlberg at the station. She took the same bus to Wiesbaden, where she had a new job as an assistant in a trading company. In John's heart, hope was growing. He would be able to see her more often!

When the bus stopped in Wiesbaden, he concentrated all his courage to ask her, "If you are in Wiesbaden, may we get together, perhaps? The Rhein-Main Base is not far from here."

"Oh, John, that would be great!"

"Good, I will let you know when I will be coming to Wiesbaden." John was happy. He had the feeling that a new life was about to begin.

"Lieutenant! John! Hello," heard John the voice of his friend, when he crossed the main gate of the base. "You have mail from home! Do not forget to take it in the mailroom!"

John smiled. Of course, he would not forget it! He adored this moment, when he took the envelope in his hand and was excited about the news from the family in Texas. He recognized his mother's handwriting on it.

My dear Johnny,

Your birthday is here and I hope this letter will find you in time to wish you happy birthday. I remember the day you were born, my adorable little baby boy, and the happiness when I took you for the first time in my arms! God bless you my son, and I wish that you find satisfaction, happiness, and peace in your life.

Peace! We waited a long time for this to come! The dark nights of fear are behind us, when I was scared of what would happen to you, Ace-of-the-sky! We waited for you after the demobilization last year. We all understand your wish to continue to fly. Do not forget though, my son, there are plenty of beautiful girls in Texas.

Grandmother was sick; she caught flu, and at her age, it was dangerous. The doctor gave her this new medicine called penicillin and she was on her feet fast. What a miracle this medicine is! Now, she is on the patio, under warm blankets.

Dad got a promotion at the factory, and that means more money. We can purchase the merchandise in the new supermarket that opened three blocks away. After the uncertainties of the war, we are all happy to go back to shopping again! In America, life is turning toward the easier side, my Johnny. In our street, everybody has found jobs here in San Antonio, or in the neighborhoods. I wish you could see the new Paseo del Rio. New constructions and sparkling lights are everywhere. It is a joy to have a walk there!

Your little brother is no longer little. A nearby factory offered him an accounting job. Your sister prepares for her graduation this year. You see we all became older. Your friend, Vincent, took over the car shop from his father. He expanded the shop and they are selling cars too. Now, that Bobby is at work, father will give him the old Ford and we will buy a new car. Can you imagine that? For years, we were not even able to dream of a new car!

Life has become more comfortable for us, my son. Do you remember the small vegetable garden in the backyard? Now, I put daisies and roses in the place of the lettuce and tomatoes. Your dad transformed the garden to a small patio, where we enjoy lemonade on the warm summer afternoons.

We miss you, my Johnny. We all hope that one day you will return to us. In the meantime, we wish you all the best and do not forget us on the other side of the world!

Kisses,

Your loving mother and the whole family

John folded the letter with care and put it back in the envelope. He took a deep breath. For a moment, he smelled the familiar scent of the Rio Grande. He loved horseback riding in the Valley on Tobasco in the company of Bucksi, his dog. The sunset colored the horizon as golden mountains and some oil tower rhythmic movements alone reminded him of civilization.

He was not homesick, however, he missed his family as much as they missed him. *Oh, home, sweet home!*

Chapter 8
The Lunch

Esther stood at her desk in the office. The secretarial job she had found did not pay well, but for her it was a real fortune. The export-import trade activity fitted her skills. She was efficient, and motivated for success. Her obliging and smiling nature earned reciprocity from her colleagues. Between young people, friendship was born fast.

Hilde came in, excited. The girl was a typical Prussian woman, tall and blonde with large bones. She was the niece of the owner, Mr. Frank.

"Esther, do you know Mister Sturm?" she asked, impatiently.

"No. I do not know... I do not remember," answered Esther uncertainly.

"He has a business in Berlin and he invited me to lunch. Would you come with me? He has an associate with him and it would be fun if you would be able to come too!"

The situation as presented by Hilde was odd, and Esther did not want to be an odd number in an odd situation. "I am not sure, Hilde... I have to finish the archive and I also have to prepare some documents for tomorrow's shipment."

"Oh, no, Esther! Don't do this to me! You know, Gerhard is a beautiful man and I hope he would care about me. You talk with his friend and I'll have him to myself. It's just for two hours!"

Esther was still hesitating.

"Esther, please... please."

"Okay, Hilde... I will survive for two hours," acquiesced Esther at the end.

When the two girls arrived in the restaurant, Gerhard Sturm was already there, waiting for them at a table. The German was indeed a beautiful young man. His Teutonic figure dominated the place: blond hair, blue eyes, large shoulders and an unusual elegance. Esther understood in an instant Hilde's enthusiasm.

"Good afternoon, ladies! I am happy you came! Please sit down!"

Gerhard Sturm was polite and considerate. He made his living through an organization on the black market. In West Berlin, he had direct connections with East and West. It was an ideal place for him.

"How is business doing, Miss Hilde? Is your uncle satisfied?"

"Yes, we are doing well these days, better than a year ago. The economy is on the rise, but you know that better than I," answered Hilde.

"I think we have an exciting period before us. Did you hear about the American Marshall Plan? Starting from 1947, plenty of materials of different sort will arrive in Europe and Germany, to the Western part of Germany, of course. Your trading company will be perhaps involved in that process."

"Perhaps..."

"I heard that the Americans delivered mules to Greece to help in the rebuilding of agriculture in the mountains," Gerhard spoke, enthusiastically. "In Italy, Fiat received a complete automated machine line from Detroit. The industrial zone of Germany might get the same treatment. We will be able to make good businesses here!"

"What do you mean?" asked Hilde. She wished for a different, more personal, discussion and hoped they would change the subject fast.

"It is simple. Stalin was convinced that the victor of the war would be the army conquering Berlin. On the contrary, the allied forces tried to put their hands on the industrial regions of Germany. Stalin was wrong. Now, the German industrial power is far from their reach. We will be able to make a good exchange with various materials in Berlin." Gerhard was not able to continue because his friend arrived.

"Hello, Hans, please sit down, we were waiting for you!"

Hans Stolzer was in his forties, round, energetic and of strong conviction, an all-time believer in democracy and freedom. He was organized and determined. He was here to settle political meetings and organizations with the democratic parties, and had a meeting with Konrad Adenauer.

The two men had many differences, but had one thing to unite them — their hatred of communism. Hans did not spend four years in Nazi camps as political prisoner to now come under another totalitarian regime. Gerhard was not able to recognize that the Soviet "Untermenschen," as inferior beings, had overcome the German armies.

"You are also in business?" asked Esther, feeling that she had to say something.

"No. I'm relocating people, helping Germans from East Germany to find a way to the Western sectors. Gerhard's organization is our liaison."

"Oh, how interesting," said Esther. His answer surprised her. She could not even conceive the existence of such an organization.

"We are organizing a new Germany, free and democratic." Hans Stolzer believed strongly in a democratic German future. "New elections will take place; we will have a government with independent politics and even a new currency. Germany will become a member of the international community of democracies. That is our goal."

"You know," intervened Gerhard, "people already have difficulty in coming to Berlin. We help them on that journey. When they are in Berlin, it is easier to pass from the Soviet sector to the British. For the moment at least."

"I would say, the Western sectors," corrected Hans. "The Gestapo arrested the commandant of the French sector, General Ganeval, when he was working for the French resistance, and interned him in the Buchenwald camp. Several German democrats, including myself, met him there. Moreover, the French Communists are strong in France and therefore they have connections on the other side. We are exploiting this aspect."

The presentation was impressive and Esther was not able to exclude herself from the impact of that exciting man. She even saw Gerhard Sturm with different eyes for joining and helping Hans Stolzer.

The lunch was joyful. For the greatest pleasure of Hilde, they began to discuss a livelier theme. The two girls got back to the office filled with amazement, however, for different reasons.

Chapter 9
The Date

The rewarding experience in the Berlin Safety Center changed John's heart. He had already discovered the joy of flying and now, after participating in that committee, he was even more impressed by the wonderful world of aviation. He wanted aviation to be part of his life after his military service.

In 1947, all Europe was talking about the Marshall Plan. John was proud that the ambitious undertaking was an American initiative. The Marshall Plan would transform Germany as well. The ruins would disappear little by little; industries would begin to function again; people would go back to work, shops and businesses would reopen and the Western part of Germany would be running again.

As a fighter pilot, John Carpenter was the king of the sky. Nevertheless, he made the decision to request transfer to the cargo handling squadron. It would be the best way to prepare for civilian life in aviation, building a new world, peaceful and generous.

The colonel was astonished at the young pilot. "Your request is unusual, Lieutenant. I never saw a fighter pilot requesting a change to transport. That's another world."

"I know, Colonel."

Two months later John Carpenter arrived in the Air Force Base in Wiesbaden for training on the C-54 transport, called "Skymaster". It was another world.

The telephone rang in the small mansion and Frau Gruber called out in her deep voice:

"Esther! Somebody's asking for you!"

Esther had good quarters in Wiesbaden. She found this room in the small mansion of Frau Gruber, where several young women rented rooms. For the first time in her life, she had a room for herself alone. In Russia, as a child, she did not have a bed for herself alone. In the concentration camp, where the survival of another day was a miracle, she imagined a future life. Every day she added something to the pictures in her head. These images linked her to an imaginary world, beautiful, splendid, and rich; they strengthened her spirit to resist the every day horrors surrounding her. Now, she thought the reality was better than the imagination of those days. She was happy.

John Carpenter was on the phone. Esther was surprised to hear that he was in Wiesbaden. She remembered the American, this tall, young person, outgoing and at the same time, a little timid and shy. John proposed a date. That was exciting! She was happy to accept it and looked forward to it.

John waited for her in downtown Wiesbaden in front of a restaurant. German guests were seldom there. Esther tried to be at her best.

"Esther, look at you! How beautiful you are!"

Esther smiled and gave him a hug. John watched her with pleasure. She had gained some weight; she was not as skinny as in Frankfurt. Her face was colored; the pale skin had been lit up. She was an agreeable picture to look at and John was proud to show up with that good-looking woman.

Esther listened to him. He had great enthusiasm. He was happy to share his feelings with her — his interest in aviation, his transfer to the transport squadron, and his vision of the future, of a peaceful world. She was thinking about her grandfather again. He wanted her to learn English from books, and now once again she was thankful to him. She was able to be here and listen to this young American, interesting and warm. She placed her hand on his forearm.

"John, you are optimistic and have vision. I love that."

He felt the warmth of her hand filling up all his body. He took her small hand in his and kissed it with affection. Esther was surprised. Their glances crossed and they immersed in a wonderful interior world made for them alone. John took her in his arms and held her tight against his chest. Her lips were wet and sweet. Their souls united in a long-lasting kiss.

Chapter 10
The Meeting

Marshal Sokolovsky stepped out from the military jeep. He stood immobile for a moment contemplating the arched windows above the front door. At the main entrance, the flags of the four allied nations flew. He took a deep breath, and with hurried steps, entered the building of the Allied Control Council in Berlin. He had clear instructions from Moscow. He had to take an open action against the Americans and the British and he would execute these instructions precisely.

The edifice of the Prussian Supreme Court housed the Allied Control Council. By some miracle, the bombardments during the battle of Berlin left the beautiful building intact. The choice of the meeting place, however, was also symbolic.

In the summer of 1944, fifty of Hitler's generals conspired to assassinate the Führer. The Nazis put the conspirators on a show-trial held in that building. These walls saw their condemnation to immediate death. The memory of the generals behaving with surprising dignity remained in the long corridors. The victory against Nazism gave them revenge.

The Allied Commanders, the American General Clay, Britain's Sir Robertson, and the French General Koenig were already in the conference room situated in the former courtroom. They did not talk; they waited in silence for the arrival of the Soviet delegation. One year ago, the American and the British merged their zones. The French finally agreed to join their plans after the communist putsch takeover in Czechoslovakia. The death of President Masaryk, founder of the Czechoslovak Republic, presented as suicide, shocked the world. This merger will divide Germany in two parts instead of four. The direct confrontation between East and West is ready to come about.

The Soviet delegation sat down and Marshal Sokolovsky opened his attack.

"Gentlemen: as an Allied Control Council member, we are requesting you to inform us about your secret meeting in London and about the decisions taken on that 'conference' as you call it."

"We do not have to inform you about anything!" responded General Clay, cautiously. The meeting and the decisions were secret. *What is it about this question? What do the Soviets know? How they are able to know about that anyway?* He watched his British counterpart and felt the same discomfort of General Sir Robertson. *Is there a mole somewhere? Or moles? That is intriguing.*

Marshal Sokolovsky opened the folder on the desk in front of him. Soviet secret agents in the middle of the British Foreign Office and Intelligence Service transmitted a detailed report to him on the London Conference. It was a comfortable feeling to be one step ahead of the opponents.

"According to your plan, you are preparing the implementation of a West German government with independent political authority under federal structure, the restructuring of the economic environment allowing free trade and enterprises, the organization of general elections and the introduction of a new currency. These measures are in contradiction with agreements set forth in the Potsdam Conference. In that respect, the Soviet Union disagrees with your initiatives and rejects your decisions."

General Clay was ready with answer.

"The American government is trying to help the European nations to get back on their feet after the war. The Secretary of State, General George Marshall is implementing a large program of financial aids for the West European countries, including Germany. That is not in contradiction with the decisions of the Potsdam Conference."

"This program is intended to transform these countries into American satellites!" General Sokolovsky deepened his attack.

"Wait a minute," intervened Sir Robertson. "These aids are also intended for the Soviet Union. You were invited to participate."

"The Soviet Union rejects these plans as we consider them as interference in our internal politics. You want to shape the political structure through the economy." Marshal Sokolovsky knew he must strengthen the Soviet standpoint now. "Once again, we request detailed information on your plans concerning Germany according to your decisions made in London. Will you give us the requested information?"

"No, we will not!"

"In that case, we do not recognize the Allied Control Council, for we may not carry out any control in the frame of that organization. We withdraw from this Council!"

With the same harsh steps he came in, General Sokolovsky left the conference room, accompanied by the Soviet delegation.

Chapter 11
Pfennigs and Groschens

Gerhard Sturm established his headquarters in the restaurant *Zum Schwarzen Wald* in the French sector. The lounge had a second entry from the backyard. He was able to settle his affairs privately. Today, he was sitting behind the big oak office desk and was playing with a pencil. The core of his group was around him. They were disciplined, military-like young men. With their obscure pasts, they participated in that organization where they felt secure and powerful at the same time. Their leather coats as soldiers' uniform fitted them well.

Dieter, his right hand man, was observing Gerhard with concern. Karl was sitting in the big armchair sipping prune schnapps. Two other persons were playing at the pool table.

"Gerhard, you are distraught. We have to organize. Concentrate on our business. This currency reform is important to us!"

"I know, Dieter. I do not see anything but good fortune for us. Do not worry!"

"I do not worry. We have to forecast, though, that our operation will be difficult for some time. The exchange rate between old Reichsmark and new D-Mark is ten-to-one. Our prices have to be adjusted."

"Dieter, this part will be simple. The Soviets introduced their new currency, the East Mark. Our temporary difficulties are coming from that fact. We have now two official currencies in Berlin. They declared an exchange rate one-to-one with the new D-Mark. It is ridiculous! We have to wait for the establishment of the fair value. We have enough financial reserves to wait two weeks."

"I agree. We have a good opportunity, Gerhard. The Soviets did not print a new banknote. They use an adhesive coupon to stick on the old Reichsmark notes. Listen, my men saw a Soviet soldier on Alexander Platz selling cigarettes for old money. He took out from his pocket coupons and glued it on the banknote. He did it in quiet, in public. We have already a source providing us with the coupons. We are in a position to have even a great number of them."

"That is a good business, you see! We will sell even the coupons! That will be an excellent business!" Gerhard was radiant.

The door opened and Anton stepped into the room. Anton was the accountant of the group. He was a man of short stature, a marionette figure. He separated his hair with precision in the middle and treated it with jelly and oil. He put his reading glasses on his forehead. He had a newspaper in his hand and was in the best mood, whistling some unrecognizable melody.

"Hello, everybody!" Anton ended the quiet silence in the room. "I made the best business deal today!"

The others turned their attention to him. They were awaiting an earthquake. Always buried in his papers, he knew all the figures and amounts and wanted to economize the tip of every candle. Far from the realty, what is the business he wants to promote?

"Yes, this is the best... I bought this newspaper for two old Reichsmarks in bank notes representing twenty new pfennigs in coins. The newspaper is fifteen pfennigs, thus I received change of five pfennigs, new pfennigs, but in the form of old groschens, which are still valid. I went to the Eastern sector, where this new five pfennigs, even in the form of old coins, are valued at fifty groschens. For these fifty groschens, I have a great choice of merchandise. Yesterday on Alexander Platz, we had a carton of Ami cigarettes for ten groschens; today it is about four groschens. For five Groschens, I would buy a whole bar of chocolate. Selling the bar of chocolate in the British sector, I will quadruple my initial investment!"

Anton felt proud and looked around him with glory. The others listened to him, astonished. Karl gulped down the schnapps, coughing. Dieter opened the mouth and his cigarette fell in his lap. Gerhard, himself, lost his composure.

"Thus, you want to make a newspaper business of five groschens and five pfennigs!"

"What? Why? I quadrupled — "

"In the end you will change twenty old Reichsmarks for one new Deutsche Mark!"

"It will be a good business if we glue the new adhesive coupon on it!"

The people present in the room began to laugh. They had heard the best joke of the day. After a moment of hesitation, Anton laughed with them.

Karl came out from his thinking. He was worried. Berlin has now two currencies, one for the Western zones and one for the Eastern zones. As a German, he was anxious about the future of his country, and in particular, about the future of his town. On the day of the currency reform, long lines were waiting at the exchange counters. Movement was near to impossible throughout the town. The shops closed soon, the newspaper carriers sold the evening papers still in the afternoon. The Berliners were calm but under the surface uncertainty was steaming as in the heart of Karl at that moment. He had broken the good-humored atmosphere.

"Good business, yes, I agree, although I do not know, how it will function. Berlin is deep inside of Soviet territory, far from the Allied zone. The Soviet-controlled press and Radio Berlin made a vehement campaign against the currency reform. The introduction of the East Mark and the clear intention of the Soviet Administration to make it the sole currency acceptable in Berlin, will link us to the Soviet zone."

"I understand, what you mean, Karl. I do not believe that, though," replied Gerhard. "I believe that the Allied Forces, the Americans in particular will not let that happen. Remember, the Americans also want to make the D-Mark the sole currency for Berlin. I think there will be a fight."

"A fight, say you?"

"Yes. I hope. The D-Mark will link Berlin, at least the Western zone of Berlin to the Allied zones of Germany. We have to fight for that. It is simple as far as I am concerned. Everybody who is against the Soviets is on my side."

"I agree," said Dieter.

"Me too," added Karl.

The two at the pool table consented with a hurrah. Dieter lit a cigarette, Karl poured another drink and the two went back to the pool game. The feeling of good businesses coming mixed with the feeling of determination.

Chapter 12
The Letter

Esther was amazed reading the letter she had received a moment ago.

According to your information request, we inform you that Avram Kohlberg, survivor of Buchenwald concentration camp, is registered with the residence on Mittelstraße 11-13, Halle, East Germany.

She was looking for her family and friends, hoping somebody survived and she would once again see cherished persons from the past. She lost hope a long time ago in part, because she learned that her family members were dead, in part, because with the passing of time, every possibility to find them had vanished.

Yes, grandfather was from Halle! When she gave all the information relating the family's history, she did not imagine that the person she would find would be a distant nephew of her grandfather. *What a pity is that he lives in East Germany!* She well knew communism; they would never be able to meet. She will not be able to go to Halle and the communists will never let him go to the West. In her childhood, the travel to the closest neighboring town or village was impossible without travel permission and passports.

All of a sudden, an idea struck her. She had lunch sometime ago with these persons from Berlin... Those who were helping others to come to the West! ... *What was his name? ... Was it Hans Stolzer?* She would find the address in the office. Through Gerhard Sturm, she would be able to get in touch with him. *Oh, yes, that is, what I would do!*

She rushed to the office and looked for the address. She wrote the letter the same day. When she received the phone call from West Berlin, she was not even surprised. She was sure of the positive answer. Now, she had to get to West Berlin. For that, she had her best friend, the man she loved — the American pilot — to lend her a hand.

"Oh, John, please help me! Would it be possible for you to take me on a transport flight to Berlin? I hear that sometimes you have also passenger!"

John was astonished. "Yes... I might... What for?" When he heard it, he understood Esther's beautiful human story.

"I know the existence of an organization in Berlin that is helping East Germans pass into the Western Occupational Territory. They will help me to find my uncle and take him out from East Germany."

"Esther, that is dangerous! You are yourself a defected Soviet citizen. You will run into trouble if they catch you!"

"They will not catch me. At first, if you fly me to Berlin, I will not meet them. The organization has a network. I will not go alone. These people know how to pass through. When we came back to Berlin, you will take us both and we will not meet them again. It is simple!"

"I think it is not as simple... nevertheless, I will help you, because I am not able to convince you not to do it."

It took some days for John to procure the necessary permission. He was proud to introduce Esther to his world and show her his flying skills. When they landed in Berlin, he had a cramp in his stomach, this well recalled, but forgotten cramp from the war. He tried to calm himself down, but was unable to free himself of that feeling of premonition.

"Everything will be okay," said Esther as if deciphering John's anxiety. "You can go ahead and organize permission for two passengers in three weeks."

Two days later, in the morning while shaving, John was listening to the radio. His thoughts went far from the bathroom. All of a sudden, the music stopped and he was stupefied at the news.

This morning, on June 24, 1948, the Soviet Army blocked all passages of West Berlin. Access is impossible from or into the city. In addition, the Soviet Administration shut down the energy supply as well. The two and half-million inhabitants are condemned to starvation. It is clear that the Soviet

Army wants to annex the city by cutting all delivery of necessary vital supply to it.

"Esther! My God, Esther is blocked in there!"

He ran to the Headquarters on the base. The military would have information that is more precise. He volunteered and was the first pilot to take off with a plane full of vital supplies in destination to West Berlin.

PART III.

BERLIN IN THOSE DAYS

Chapter 13
The Leaders

Ernst Reuter opened the door of the conference room in the Allied Control Council Building with a firm hand. In his other hand, he held the walking stick he still used because of a grave injury in World War I, where he served on the Eastern Front. While in Russian captivity there, he embraced communism and even became commissar in the German autonomy of the Volga. After his homecoming, he took a leading role in the German communist party. It did not last for long though. He harshly criticized the growing Bolshevik influence, and they expelled him. Arrested by the Nazis several times, he had to emigrate to Turkey. Berliners elected him Lord Mayor of Berlin. The Soviets vetoed the election and never accepted him in this position.

He arranged the beret he wore everyday as did Pablo Picasso, his favorite artist, and took a deep breath. Today, he had to continue to fight with all his conviction to preserve democracy and freedom in a town in the middle of controversial interests.

The military commanders, General Clay, General Sir Robertson and General Koenig, were already at the table waiting for him, while having an agitated discussion. In fact, they had a dangerous situation to manage.

"Thank you, for coming as quickly as you did, Mister Reuter" began General Lucius Clay. "As you are aware, in the last weeks we have had many troubles in rail and road traffic," he continued. "Today, according to the communiqué received from Marshal Sokolovsky in person, the Soviet Military Commandant closed all access from and into West Berlin. The Soviets pleaded that the overused Helmstedt-Berlin railway needs maintenance from top to bottom. They informed us, moreover, about disturbances in the power station Golpa-Zschornewitz, which delivers electricity to the Western sectors of Berlin. The explanation is the same, technical difficulties."

"And do you believe that?" inquired Ernst Reuter.

"Of course not. All these measures are intended to drive us out of Berlin."

Willy Brandt, the young and energetic associate of Ernst Reuter smiled. The young man accompanied Reuter everywhere; they worked closely together.

"Generals, the greatest threat to the freedom of Europe lies in the expansionist foreign policy of the Soviet Union and in communism." Willy Brandt spoke with the enthusiasm popular with young politicians. "The preservation of freedom in West Germany requires close collaboration with the Western protective powers. Iron determination has been the sole wall of defense against the new totalitarianism at the disposition of Berliners in the last three years. The moment now has come, where this determination is not enough and where the will and force of the Berliner needs the support of the free and democratic world."

Reuter stopped him, placing his hand on Brandt's forearm, and continued his own intervention.

"I would like to thank you for your support and courageous action in introducing the Western Deutsche Mark to West Berlin despite the strong opposition of the Soviets. The introduction of the new Western currency links Berlin to the Western democracies. The Soviets know that. The Soviets want to have all Berlin under their influence and their plan is the evacuation of the Allied forces from the Western sectors."

"Yes, we know it. Let me ask you this, Mister Reuter, will the German people and the inhabitants of West Berlin be able to make sacrifices for a system they do not even know?"

"What do you mean?" asked Ernst Reuter, astonished.

General Koenig was surprised. The French General did not expect such a philosophical remark from the American. The French people suffered horrible experiences and paid ultimate sacrifices in both World Wars. The French government was ready to join the British and the Americans in their London propositions, but had reservations about the German question. The ability to establish democracy in Germany was a continuous worry for political circles in France.

"Yes, that is true," said General Koenig taking over from his American counterpart. "The Germans lived in a monarchy until the end of World War I. In 1933, you passed under a dictatorship. Between monarchy and dictatorship your memories of democracy are limited to a short period from 1919 to 1933."

"Generals, we want to establish true democracy in Germany. You must not doubt this. Moreover, we are convinced that if you want to save democracy in Europe, you have to save it in Berlin!" said Willy Brandt, with vehemence.

"What are your intentions now?" asked Ernst Reuter.

"In fact, we have already begun our actions," responded General Sir Brian Robertson. "Our Dakotas are taking off at regular intervals delivering vital supplies to our warehouses in the British sector. We will open these warehouses for the inhabitants of West Berlin."

"We are organizing the same," underlined General Clay. "We stocked up some reserves in the last weeks and we will open these reserves for the Berliners. We will use our fleet of C-47s and the two Skymasters, which we have available now. I intend to request more planes for the airlift."

"The situation in the French sector is difficult," explained General Koenig. "We do not have significant reserves. The French government, however, will support the actions of our allies. We support the creation of the air bridge."

General Clay had to obtain the approval of the Berliners. This point was of particular importance to the American Administration.

"We wanted to have this meeting with you, for no action would be effective without the support from the people of the town under siege." General Clay wanted to make clear this point. "There are two and half million inhabitants in the Western sectors including allied military personnel. To keep the town alive, we need about thirteen thousand tons of food and fuel per day. Our actual capacity is around four thousand tons at best. It represents between a thousand and twelve hundred calories per day per person."

"I am ready to try an airlift," continued the American General. "I cannot guarantee it will work. I am sure even at best, people are going to be cold and are going to be hungry. If the people of Berlin will not stand with us, it will fail. I do not want to go into this unless I have your assurance that the people will be heavily in approval," told General Clay.

"You take care of the airlift. I will take care of the Berliners," answered Ernst Reuter, calmly and leaned back in his seat. The participants read the determination on his face. Pride filled Willy Brandt's heart. *Yes, we will,* he thought.

"That's good enough for me!" finished General Clay, with the determination of a soldier.

Chapter 14
The Demonstration

Esther arranged her room in the small hotel. She planned to stay one, or no more than two weeks in Berlin, but she wanted to feel at home. Her meeting with the people helping to get to her uncle and to come with him back to Berlin was a success and excitement filled her heart.

She knew the Soviets well. All her thoughts were exact. Harassments and controls were taking place, the moving and traveling in Eastern Germany was a complicated and risky undertaking. She needed the help of these people to carry out her mission.

She was ready to leave, when suddenly, she heard running steps on the staircase and somebody knocked on the door. It was Hans Stolzer.

"Esther! The Soviets put Berlin under blockade!" Hans Stolzer was shaken up. "There is no access from and into the city! They want to break us by hunger and privation."

She felt a growing nervousness. In her heart she knew, though, the Americans would not let it happen. John will not let it happen...

They went together to the restaurant *Zum Schwarzen Wald* to gather information through Gerhard, who was the best-informed person in town. While they discussed in the lounge of the restaurant, they heard a car on the street with loudspeaker making the announcement:

Come to a meeting at the Reichstag and show your determination against this blockade. Support our mayor and our freedom.

They thought to use Gerhard's car, but had to stop and park it. Five hundred cars were waiting in line in the East-West exit — American, English, French, Czechs, Swiss, Polish, and many cars from

East Germany — that had covered their license plates under bands of newspaper.

As they approached the neighborhood of the German Parliament, the Reichstag, people were gathering all around. Firms and companies in some districts of West Berlin closed the business at two o'clock in the afternoon. Inhabitants of entire house blocks marched together. Factories and offices transported their personnel on trucks to the demonstration. Hundreds of young people crowded windows and roof of the Reichstag. On the ruins of the Opera House and on the former military headquarters pressed thousands of onlookers.

Companies of British Military Police along with German Police officers from the Western sectors tried to maintain order. In front of them, Soviet soldiers fortified the detachment of police officers from the Eastern Sector.

Three hundred thousand people gathered at the Reichstag. Esther never saw so many people together. Fear was in her heart, but at the same time, she was proud to be here. All of a sudden, she understood, these people share as one all the principles, which governed her. They had different past, different experiences, but these principles of freedom and democracy were the link between them. That is the future; that has to be the future for all of Europe...

They saw the Mayor of Berlin, Ernst Reuter, in the company of General Lucius Clay, commander of the American Occupational Army in Germany. Loudspeakers transmitted the discourse of the orators. Ernst Reuter stepped up to the stand and spoke with conviction to the crowd.

"We have to stop the Soviet expansionism to avoid the establishment of a system well known by all of us, where ordering and obeying will bring back our old 'friends' — prisons and concentration camps! Today, no diplomat or general will speak or negotiate. Today, the people of Berlin will make their voices heard. People of America, England, France, Italy, and the people of the world — look at this city! Do not abandon this city and its people! You should not abandon it!" said Ernst Reuter on the stand.

The American General took over the microphone. "We will not allow the people in West Berlin to starve! We are in Berlin in compliance with international agreement reached after the war regarding Germany. The Soviet attempt to take the population of Berlin hostage is a clear violation of these agreements! We will build up an air bridge to Berlin in order to provide the town with vital supplies. Not even another war would drive us out from Berlin!"

The speech was followed and accompanied by applause and confirming whispering. They lived the rare moments of history when the same strong spirit unifies leaders and masses, and feelings are flowing between them without barriers.

"Even the strong winter will not force us to our knees!"

"Did you hear, the Royal Air Force is already in the sky?"

"Will they, in fact, be able to feed us by air?"

"The Americans will support us!"

"They threw many bombs on our heads only some years ago, why would they not be able to throw as many supplies now?"

Esther was in the middle of a moving mass. People were shoving and trampling each other. She had a fear that perhaps the crowd would overrun her. An old man with his stick in hand... a father holding tight his little son... a woman with glazed eyes... young people yelling... couples holding each others hands... men with dark determination on their faces...

An invisible hand directed the mass toward Brandenburg Gate; the majestic architecture was the natural frontier between the Eastern and Western part of the town. On the top of it, next to the group of statues, the Red Flag of the Soviets. An armed Soviet military jeep arrived to carry out the sentry relief at that moment. Boos, shouting and whistles accompanied them. Agitation was at its highest.

"What are they looking here for?"

"They have to stay in their sector!"

The Soviets lifted their arms and now the whistles transformed into a hurricane. Flying stones hit the Soviet jeep. The British Military Police protected them and helped them to the Brandenburg Gate, avoiding confrontation. Soviet soldiers with machine guns aimed toward the demonstrators rushed from the sentry post. The stones continued to fly. One British officer tried to negotiate with the Soviets to stop menacing their weapons.

Two youngsters, pushed by the overwhelming excitement, scaled the monument and tore down the flag. The crowd ripped it to shreds and continued to stone the Soviets. A new platoon of Soviet soldiers arrived on a truck, accompanied with boos, shouting and whistles. The Eastern police officers began to beat up whomever they could. They arrested one young man. The excitement because of the arrest was enormous. A commissar shouted intention to fire warning shots. The people answered with stones once again. The Soviets opened fire. Screaming and yelling — Blood and suffering — Tears and shrieking.

"Calm down! They are waiting for an opportunity to open armed hostilities!"

"Do not give them the chance or possibilities to attack us!"

Soviet soldiers climbed the monument and brought a new red flag. Two Soviet officers tried to pull two Western police officers from their car. A British car came to their assistance and pursued the Soviet jeep. While Soviet and British officers negotiated at Brandenburg Gate, the crowd pressed into the Zoo and Stresemann street in the American sector fleeing from the fire of machine guns.

When Esther saw the young German dead on the ground, she cried. For the first time in her life she wanted to do something — to be part of this movement and share this particular experience with the people she did not know. However, she knew that a free life comes at a price, holding out against hostilities and privation. Perhaps, all that she had lived through until now will have a purpose and her past suffering will serve to build a victory.

She did not sleep that night. She was sitting in her bed, thinking. *What shall I do? For sure, I will stay in Berlin.* She would not be able to stay here though, in the hotel; it would be too expensive. She also needed a job. They would need people to organize this entire airlift. They would need people at the airports, Tempelhof in the American sector, and Gatow in the British zone. They would also need people, perhaps, in the city hall. She had to check out all these possibilities.

When she found a job, she would look to rent a small studio. Perhaps in Tempelhof. She would be close to John... John has to come...

She needed him. His tender presence would be securing. His strong arms are protecting. When she fell asleep, tender and sweet dreams accompanied her where the warmness of love fulfilled all of her desires.

Chapter 15
The Battlefield

General Clay, a Southerner, graduate from West Point and army engineer, was working on his report. On his shoulder strap, four stars shined. He earned the four stars through his achievements far from enemy lines. He requested his transfer to combat several times during the war. His organizational skills were important and he had to exercise his talent to ensure the logistics and maintenance of the army. He became a General without even going to a battle.

Germany, and especially Berlin, was the one place where the Soviet troops and the troops of the free world came into direct confrontation. Demobilization had left the U.S. Army and the U.S. Air Force in Europe with around sixty thousand volunteer troops. Nearly four hundred-thousand Soviets were opposing them supported by a good tactical air force. In the case of a shouting war, the Soviets would be at a considerable advantage. Now, the General arrived, where he always wanted to be — on the battlefield.

He did not believe this to be a cold war. He believed the Soviets were testing the conviction and determination of the Allied countries. *Are they ready to transform these cold war hostilities into a hot war? Are they looking to launch World War III?* It would be simple to verify that. The Allied forces would have to send an armed convoy from West Germany to Berlin. If the Soviets attack them, they want the war; if they let them pass, it's the end of the blockade.

He called his adjutant. "More coffee, please!"

"General, that will be the third pot today! You did not eat a normal lunch, you are only drinking coffee."

The general was a hardworking man, an always-turned up dynamo. He was able to maintain his concentration during long hours, extracting the essence of a memo at a glance while eating a single sandwich at the corner of his desk and downing an impressionable quantity of coffee.

Knowing him as a charge-taker who brings chaotic situations to working order, General Eisenhower sent for him after the D-Day to clear up the war-torn Port of Cherbourg, a port vital to the Allied flow of supplies. The General remembered the entangled harbor. He needed twenty-four hours to stabilize its situation. Two days later, the port facilities were functioning with speed and efficiency. Now, he would need all his skills, enthusiasm and tenacity to face the days and weeks ahead. Destiny placed him in a unique position with unique challenges. The time has come to meet with history.

He was familiar with aircraft and airports. In the Defense Airport Program in 1940 and 1941, he had responsibility on the staff of General McArthur to enlarge and improve two hundred and seventy-seven airports, and to build one hundred and ninety-seven new ones. Today, he must find airplanes. He would take care of airports later.

Lucius Clay knew the one man who would help him — Curtis LeMay, General of U.S. Air Force in Europe. LeMay's fame in the field of aviation was solid. During the war, he was able to mold successful fighting units where no resources were available. General Clay was sure LeMay would be the man to understand and support his decision to implement this airlift. General Clay picked up the phone and dialed his number.

"General, we need airplanes to lift vital supplies to Berlin."

In war, Curtis LeMay was determined to win as fast as possible. In peace, he was determined to make war appear so terrible that it would not take place again. He was ready for combat every day. Now, that day had come. He would launch the formidable power of the U.S. Air Force in a battle over Berlin to save the two and half million inhabitants.

"You got it. I will order the immediate implementation of missions. What do you need exactly and what are your provisions?"

"We are concluding the plans. It is clear that our biggest problem is coal. Coal is critical. Would the Air Force be able to deliver coal to Berlin?"

"General, the Air Force is able to deliver anything," answered Curtis LeMay. His round face was in marble. His small eyes were dazzling from determination. That will be a prestigious mission for the newborn Air Force, converted to a separate military arm a short time ago.

After hanging up, LeMay first ordered a full-scale alert and put all pilots and crews on the task. After that, he began to analyze the situation. The Air Force in Europe had two troop carrier squadrons equipped with one hundred-two C-47s each capable of hauling three tons of cargo. They also had two Skymasters in Europe, each hauling ten tons. The General knew the British Royal Air Force was in no better shape having only forty Dakotas, and the French had almost no planes at all to offer. The struggle in Indochina preoccupied France that had almost nothing in the way of air transport available in Europe. The airlift will need more planes. He launched a request to transfer to Europe all available Skymasters. They had to come from Alaska, Hawaii, Guam, Massachusetts, Panama, California, Japan and Texas.

Yeah, we are going to keep this city alive, he thought and leaned back in his seat with determination.

Chapter 16
Spying the Skies

Marshal Sokolovsky installed his headquarters in Babelsberg, a suburb of Potsdam, near Berlin. He was not in Potsdam at the time that Marshal Zhukov represented the Soviet Union there at the signing of the German surrender. During the war, the two men had their differences, and Zhukov emerged victorious from it. At this time, General Sokolovsky had to return to the Ukraine front. Later, after his nomination as Marshal of the Soviet Union and Commander in Chief of Germany, and as a personal revenge on Marshal Zhukov, he established his headquarters not far from the small palace where the German surrender was signed.

Marshal Sokolovsky came from a fervent Christian family. He was a schoolteacher in his village when he entered the Red Army at the age of twenty-one, and distinguished himself during the civil war. His precise quotations from the bible made him well known in the Frunse Military Academy, the West Point of the Soviet Union. Now, he was in his wood-decorated, aristocratic office in the company of his military officers, and on the phone on a conference call with Vyacheslav Molotov, Foreign Minister of the Soviet Union.

"Comrade Minister," began Marshal Sokolovsky with a firm voice, "our message to the Allies is clear. They must be able to understand the symbolic meaning of the blockade. We did not choose the date by coincidence. This date is exactly seven years after Adolf Hitler launched Operation Barbarossa, the invasion of the Soviet Union. This date also is shortly over three years since the Battle of Berlin. For us, the blockade is the battle aimed to drive them out from Berlin. When they are out, we will be able to launch the next step, driving them out from Germany."

"Comrade Marshal, we know that," answered Molotov. The pompous manners of Sokolovsky annoyed him. "Let us speak about this airlift. What is the situation?"

"I do not believe in the success of an airlift. It is not possible to supply a city of two and half million inhabitants through the air, over an extended time. Moreover, Berlin is, from the military standpoint, indefensible." Marshal Sokolovsky was calm and believed in a quick victory.

"Do not underestimate the adversary, Comrade," underlined Molotov. "The Americans are making Berlin a symbol of the American intent, and this fact is able to push them to the extreme."

"I agree in theory with that analysis, Comrade Minister," answered Marshal Sokolovsky. "Please keep in mind, however, the battle of Stalingrad. The Germans implemented a massive airlift there. We saw its complete failure for they were not able to bring in even three hundred tons per day. Berlin needs several thousands of tons per day! With the miserable Berlin weather approaching, we have just to wait and the blockade will succeed."

Molotov had other concerns.

"Comrade General, as you know the Allies implemented a counter blockade, thus we are not receiving supplies vital for our economy. Certainly you are aware of the difficult economic issues in the Soviet occupational territory in Germany. It is important for us to succeed with the blockade, and fast."

"We are aware of these facts, Comrade Minister. The capitalists want to do business. I am confident they will come back to negotiation. We will have them by their money!"

"I am not as optimistic, Comrade Marshal."

Silence ensued for a moment on both ends of the phone. Foreign Minister Molotov broke the silence.

"Do we have any information? How many tons they are hauling per day?"

"We had a spy in an apartment in front of Tempelhof airport, and we had clear notification on the tonnages. Alas, the information was useless. Our spy reported huge tonnages, which were a clear exaggeration. We do not believe that this performance is possible. My intelligence officer already fired the spy. We will put another agent on the task."

"Very good, Comrade."

"I have another concern, Comrade Minister. The Americans fortified their fighting strength. According to the information collected by our military intelligence, they transferred B-29 bombers to England. A squadron of Thunderbolt fighters also arrived in the region. We have to fortify our position in return, I believe."

"You are not planning to bring tanks out into the streets, are you?" asked Minister Molotov, nervously.

"No, not in the streets... My intention is just to move them closer to Berlin."

"No, do not do that! Let us wait for a moment. If you bring out your tanks, they will bring out their tanks. It is better to resolve this issue by using diplomatic language. Hold to our 'technical difficulties' and wait for the airlift to fail."

"We are able to institute harassments in the corridors," proposed the Marshal.

"Yes, but you have to stay within the limit of the written covenant."

The conference call finished with an optimistic tone. *What happens to Berlin happens to Germany; what happens to Germany happens to Europe. The Soviet Union is marching toward a victory. Today Berlin, tomorrow the whole of Europe will be ours,* thought Molotov with certainty.

Chapter 17
The Decision

When Esther entered the city hall, full chaos reigned there. People were running all over the place, phones were ringing, doors were clacking, and people were waiting in line at the counters. She approached a woman working at the counter who, behind her glasses, had a serious expression and looked official.

"I'm looking for some work. Could you help me, please?" The woman led her through crowded corridors to a clerk.

"We have high unemployment in Berlin nowadays, you know," said the clerk in the employment office. "What type of job are you looking for?"

"What do you have available? I was a secretary in Wiesbaden... If you have something outside of an office though, I will be happy... Perhaps on the airports... I speak English."

"English? That is interesting. Yes, we have some openings at the airports. The Americans are requesting several interpreters." The clerk made a quick decision. "Let us try it out. When will you be able to begin? Right away?"

Esther found herself at the airport in two hours. She was in an airport for the first time in her life when she flew here with John. That was memorable. She had been afraid, and spent a lot of energy to hide her apprehension before John. She fell in love with flying though in the first ten minutes after takeoff. John showed her the countryside below them. It was amazing! She was able to view far beyond the horizon to the forest and river. The people and cars, town and villages were as small toys in the hands of children. She understood why John adored flying as much as he did. Arriving at Tempelhof, she followed him and was not aware of the neighborhood. This time was different.

Now, her senses and her mind tried to catch everything around her. *That is the place and those are the peoples who will save Berlin and the democracy,* she thought.

As a parade field, Tempelhof witnessed the first demonstration flights by the Frenchman, Armand Zipfel, followed by Orville Wright at the turn of the twentieth century. Tempelhof's reputation in aviation was born, however its designation as an airport did not arrive until 1926. The Nazis ordered the replacement of the old terminal by a new one of granite construction, still known as one of the largest such structure built worldwide. Its purpose was to promote the overwhelming superiority of the Germans during the Olympic Games of Berlin in 1936. Fine and elegant people passed through the salon of the terminal. During the war, a new building was added for the assembly lines of bombers and fighters.

The architecture and the construction amazed Esther. The giant hangars were crowded. The planes, small as birds in the sky, are enormous iron monsters on the ground. She had difficulty in finding her way to the offices. The American Army was in bursting over. Reinforcements for the maintenance troops arrived at first, and were quick to organize servicing of several planes in line at the same time.

The Chief Maintenance Officer, Major Tom Crawley, was an experienced soldier, but had little time to put the ground organization in motion for the most important airlift operation ever seen.

He directed Esther. "Call Airport Administration. We need workers for offloading. We have to cooperate with the Mayor's office concerning shipments to the different districts in the town. What are their needs; what are their plans? Request confirmation for the trucks. We need hundreds of empty trucks here. Organize a meeting for me with the railroad. We need an administrative follow-up of the shipments. Request civil personal to register incoming and outgoing deliveries..."

Esther was running after him trying to note everything, but he left her behind. She almost lost the breath, her small hat was hanging on her neck, and her hair-do was gone with the wind. Thanks to God, Major Tom Crawley stopped several times because soldiers requested instructions and she was able to take control of herself. When they arrived at the small office, she fell right on the seat.

"Major, Major. Please, I am a friend of Lieutenant John Carpenter, a pilot and I would like to know when he arrives... He has to come..."

Tom Crawley, at the doorstep, turned slowly and for some moments observed Esther in silence. *What a nice girl!* Her face was red from running in the hangar. Her big, green eyes penetrated him. *Yes, these two young things are in love, for sure.*

"I will pass the word. What is your name?"

"Esther Kohlberg."

"Good. I will pass the word, Miss Kohlberg."

After recovering her breath, Esther examined the small office. Chaos reigned here, for the office of a military commander. *Men are not able to organize themselves*, she observed. She arranged the desk, and began to phone and settle the open questions according to the request of the Major. By luck, her work experience in the Trading Company in Wiesbaden helped her. She found a newspaper on the desk and hurriedly looked over the rentals. Now, that she had the job, she had to find a small apartment and organize an everyday life in that town under siege.

Nevertheless, for now, she had to finish that long day. It would take two hours to get to the hotel this evening. The power shortage imposed a severe limitation to the traffic of streetcars, and the simplest journey became a real expedition. As soon as Major Tom Crawley returns and she hands over the requested reports, she had to leave at once.

John received his orders and waited in the office while the loading team prepared his Skymaster. His team, Josh, the second pilot, Chuck, the navigator, and Garry, the radio technician, were waiting with him. Their faces reflected the seriousness of the situation.

"What do you think, Lieutenant, is it World War Three?"

"I do not know... I hope not. This is a humanitarian effort; we do not want to let all these people starve!"

"I dislike the Soviets. They are untrustworthy."

"They are rude. We all heard about the brutalities of the Soviet Army. They raped all the women they found. My girlfriend spent three days under the couch. When Soviet soldiers entered the room, the whole family sat down on the couch."

"I heard they were looking for alcohol. They even drank the toilet water because it contained alcohol!"

"I heard they stole all the wrist watches! They had a forearm full of watches!"

"Do not be foolish," intervened John. "They are human beings, but they do not know how to live and do not know anything about freedom and democracy. They behave in the same way as other armies behaved with them. They had Father Tsars before and now they have Generalissimo Stalin. I have pity for them."

The loading got finished and John was running to the plane. He jumped into the pilot seat and began to perform the usual checklist.

"Hey, old chap, what is that hurry? We were not able to catch you up!"

The crew was complete. They were joking, laughing, but John did not hear them. The others were staring to each other with astonishment. It seemed, that was a special day...

Yes, indeed, it was a special day. In their hearts, they felt it. Now, a new form of war was in the beginning stages. Nobody knew where and how it would finish. Today, they transported food and vital goods. What is about tomorrow though? Would they transport bombs? They contemplated the sky. Would the Soviets permit the airlift to function? They anticipated attacks, or at least some disturbances.

In John's head, the discussions from three years ago came alive. At that time in history no one thought about preserving the air for military reasons. They wanted secure airspace for everyone. The smiling face of Pete was present in his spirit. He perished in an accident giving birth to that written covenant, which represents now the safeguard for two and half million people. It is indeed amazing how life and death find purposes through the mill of time!

Chuck was the first to signal the enemy fighter.

"Lieutenant! There — That's a Soviet plane!"

"Yes, you are right! It's a Yak." John recognized the plane at once.

"Do you think they are going to attack?" Garry, the navigator was nervous. John laughed.

"No, not at all! They are not attacking! They are following our flight. They want to intimidate us."

"How can you be sure of that?"

"Did you forget that I was a fighter pilot? I participated in air combat. This Yak will not attack us. They just want to disturb us."

John observed the Soviet fighter. The distance between them was less than ninety feet. According to the international agreement, they had no right to be so close. All of a sudden, the Yak turned and made a nosedive around them. Chuck and Garry were surprised. John gripped the wheel. He concentrated on the altitude and maintained a straight line. The old reflex from the war came back with surprising rapidity.

The crew felt relieved when Tempelhof airport came into sight. When John made the necessary maneuvers for landing, his heart began to beat faster. He had to find out what was happening to Esther. He knew the hotel where she was staying. He had no time to go there though. His flight back to the base was scheduled in a short time. He would be able to call the hotel and leave a message for her. Perhaps, he would be lucky and would catch her there. It would be nice to hear her voice.

He jumped out of the airplane, when he heard his name.

"Lieutenant John Carpenter! Do you know Lieutenant John Carpenter?"

"Yes, I am John Carpenter."

"Oh, hello. Major Tom Crawley wants to see you. Please come with me."

Tom Crawley was overwhelmed with the ground organization of the airlift. He contemplated the young pilot for a moment. *What a handsome young man is this one! The girl is beautiful too.* He was smiling but he did not show his amusement.

"Private, accompany the Lieutenant to my office. We will have a meeting there."

"Major, I have a couple of phone calls to make. May I do it from your office?"

"Yes, of course. My secretary will help you, if you need assistance."

"Thank you." John felt relieved. If the secretary would help him, he would somehow find Esther.

The young woman was arranging some documents, when John entered the office. When she turned round, John's heart stopped beating for a second.

"Esther!"

"John!"

They fell in each other's arms kissing and holding each other tight. The world vanished around them. They understood at that moment how deeply they loved each other and how important this love was for them.

"Esther! I will take you back to Wiesbaden. I have the authorization. You will not be able to stay here. I want to know you are safe."

"No, John. I will stay here. For the first time in my life, I made a choice. Until now, things happened to me, and I was not in a position to do anything about it. I was too young or the situation was too hopeless. I lost my family. I saw my friends die. I survived because I wanted to, and still today, I did not yet realize how I did it. I profited from the occasion that life presented to me after the war to be on the American side."

Esther spoke with fervor. The words came from her heart. She was very convincing.

"Now, this time is different." The determination heated up her voice. "I want to be here. I want to do something, I want to be useful and I want to share this period with these people. I do not want the Soviets here and I do not want to let them institute their total regime. The single thing I am able to do about it, is to stay here. Now, this is my time and my way to pay back and take my revenge by standing strong and staying here."

John was staring at her, filled with admiration. *What a wonderful human being she is! She was right. This is the time to measure courage and conviction.* He knew it; he felt it. In the cockpit some hours ago, during the short flight to Berlin, disordered thoughts came to his mind, and he was not able to put the words in sentences. He felt in his spirit alone that challenging times are coming to him, in his personal life but also for that fragile peace where a new world is trying to be born. Esther expressed his own feelings perfectly, and that was the truth.

After the war, seeing Germany in ruins, he felt responsible. Now, the time had come to get rid of his personal demons and to do something for the Germans who merited living in a free society. *My God, it sounds like a mission!* This is something that they will be able to share with each other! His heart beat faster. *Yes, this is it, an ideal to share in common!* This ideal will unite them forever. He wanted to earn her admiration. He took her hands in his and covered them with soft kisses. She smiled tenderly. He peered deep into her eyes.

"Esther Kohlberg, I love you."

"Oh, John, I love you too."

They were holding each other tight when Tom Crawley entered the office. The tough soldier knew the power of love. He contemplated the two young persons with interest.

"I see the meeting has concluded."

"Oh, thank you," said Esther blushing.

"Your plane is getting ready, Lieutenant. I think you intend to take her out from here."

"I intended, but she wants to stay here."

Tom Crawley was astonished. *Life is full of surprises. This girl has character.*

"Esther, I will find you here next time…"

"I will wait for you."

Tom Crawley was aware of the order in the office and on his desk. *This girl is efficient.* He noted the newspaper on the desk opened at the classified listings. Esther had marked some rental ads in red.

"Miss Kohlberg, are you looking for rentals?"

"Yes, I am."

"Perhaps, I will be able to help you. The Army has some connections to rentals for civilian personnel."

"Thank you, Major."

Two days later Esther set down her luggage in a mansion and she felt relieved. The mansion belonged to a large family. Her room was small, but comfortable. The Soviets shut down electricity early, but the moonlight shone into the room giving it a romantic touch. Determination and love filled her heart. Tomorrow would be a beautiful day.

Chapter 18
The Journalist

The young man entering the building of the station "Radio In American Sector", known as RIAS, was an American journalist. He wore a dark blue jeans and a checkered shirt. He bought his leather jacket from a pilot after the war and he enjoyed the comfortable feeling. A camera was hanging around his neck. He was a freelance reporter working for American newspaper and broadcasting companies. He liked the status of being freelance. He felt free to conduct his investigations without caring about company policies. This freedom would be precious now.

"Hi. I'm Bob Howard. I'm a journalist. May I speak with the Director, please?"

Colonel William Heimlich received all journalists with the same courtesy. It was important to maintain the international interest for Berlin and it was even more important to support the morale of the Berliners.

"You know, Bob, the Soviets declared this blockade while they conduct a real war of communication for several years. They are masters of disinformation. Radio Berlin is one of their leading instruments. For that reason, our mission here is of high importance."

The Soviet Army reinstalled Radio Berlin with immediate effect after the battle of Berlin. The Soviets and their allies, the German communists, controlled the huge building with the most powerful radio transmitter in Europe. The building was located in the American sector, but the Soviets refused any participation in its management.

The Allies, frustrated with this situation, had no choice but to launch a new radio station and "Radio In American Sector", RIAS, was born. Colonel Heimlich was proud to give detailed information to all persons interested in the activities of the RIAS. He spoke about "his station" with enthusiasm.

"At the beginning we had a small one-thousand-watt transmitter, and broadcast for just a few hours a day. The weak signal limited the audience. One year ago, the transmitter capacity increased to twenty thousand watts and the airtime to thirteen hours per day. Now, we are able to broadcast to a radius of around one-hundred-twenty miles. General Clay authorized us to answer Communist anti-Western propaganda. He charged me, an American, to head the station, and by that fact to withstand the worst of any Soviet criticism for the RIAS German staff."

"Now, during the blockade, what is your mission?" asked Bob Howard.

"RIAS began to broadcast twenty four hours a day after the beginning of the blockade with immediate effect. We provide all types of emergency information with respect to daily power allocations and availability of rationed items."

"It sounds great, but the Berliners have electricity for two or three hours and for the most part, in the night. How are they able to listen to you?"

"They wake up in the middle of the night for washing, ironing, cooking, and also listening to RIAS. In Berlin, life is, without doubt, nightlife. You will experience it yourself. We put also loudspeakers on mobile trucks and send them to various neighborhoods to get information out to those who need it. On the other hand, our audience is growing in the Soviet sector, where we are the only free source of information."

Colonel Heimlich was proud and enthusiastic. He introduced the American broadcasting technique on the theory that if the audience is not here, nobody is able to convince them of anything. Get people to listen! He gave them good entertainment and solid news to depend upon. As a soldier, he was completely satisfied.

"I have also to underline, that we also have a military function attributable to our powerful transmitter. We provide a navigation signal for the airlift pilots to guide them to Berlin."

Bob Howard was impressed. The American people became passionate about Berlin and the situation of the Berliners. How is somebody able to accept the hostage-taking of a whole town? The Americans at home began to organize collections of food, textiles and other goods. Help from the American nation was already flowing into Berlin. Bob, armed with information, arrived to Berlin to see, to live, and to inform directly from the heart of events.

"Bob, you are always welcome, if we are able to help you with anything, do not hesitate to ask! We support free journalism!"

"Thanks, Willy!"

Bob left the RIAS building, amazed. One meeting was enough to find the much-needed local connection, his local base in Berlin. All of a sudden, something had fallen on his head. What was that? He directed his gaze toward the sky, where the planes passed in line and noticed that small parachutes were coming down. He received one of them on his head. He opened it with curiosity. A candy bar! He heard the yelling of children on the street. They were running after the small parachutes. Their joy was without limit. Bob gave his newfound candy bar to one of them.

An American pilot throwing bonbons, chocolates and chewing gum over Berlin! What a story! He had to find out more about that. That would be his first story. *Life is wonderful!*

Chapter 19
The Family

The Eberhardt villa stood proud in the fine suburb of Berlin. It was once an elegant district, but the war left its mark on the neighborhood. The Eberhardt villa had some luck during the bombing. Bombs fell in the garden or on the street. They destroyed or damaged many mansions, but none of them struck the villa. After the bombing, during the last battle of Berlin, machine guns, cannons and grenades added to the destruction. The elegant decorations on the façade cracked and all the windows broke. In the last three years, they repaired the roughcast on several occasions and restored the windows one by one. Life became more comfortable in the mansion, but the former splendor was gone forever.

Gerd Eberhardt sat in the garden and enjoyed the warm sunshine. The smell of spring was still in the air, but the blooming summer was shining through the leaves. The man was in his forties, but appeared nearer to sixty. The long years he spent on the front as a surgeon marked him. He always served on the front line, in particular two years under Leningrad on the Eastern front. His life did not differ from that of any soldier, and he suffered injuries several times. He had his feet frozen in the strong Russian winter and lost three toes during the retreat. He was the single man of the family who survived and came back home.

"What a beautiful afternoon," said Trudi Eberhardt as she placed the tray with coffee and cake on the table. She was thirty-five, but some gray was already mixed in with her brown hair. She became the head of the family during the war. The Eberhardts had four children, although only three were alive: Johann, the eldest son; Anna, their daughter; and little Fritz. Their last, an adorable baby boy, conceived during her husband's furloughs, contracted a common cold in the bitter winter of 1944. She was not able to do anything for him. No one was able to. In the strong bombing during the battle of Berlin, it was impossible to get any assistance or medicine, and the child died in silence. Trudi learned how to transform nothing into something when the survival of the family was at stake.

She had an idea to repair the servant apartment and create a separate living area. In the neighborhood, the Eberhardt Villa was the first to have a telephone line in the 1920s. With the telephone and the separate room, she obtained a listing with the American Army. The rental fees were welcome income for the family and helped them to overcome everyday difficulties.

"Good evening, Esther! Do you want to share coffee and cake with us?"

"Yes, Trudi. Thank you! You are crazy though to prepare these luxuries. We are struggling with the minimum to survive and you made coffee and cake."

"I know, Esther. These are the last luxuries that we are able to afford. I want us to remember something. The memories of this coffee and cake will help us to get through the coming weeks and even perhaps months of privation."

Esther regarded Trudi with admiration. Memories and imagination of a better life gives strength of resistance. The two women had sympathy for each other from the first moment. Esther was much more mature than her age and Trudi became more patient and understanding during the difficult time of war. The age difference was more a bridge than a separation between them.

"Where are the children?"

"They are at the playground. All the children of the neighborhood are together. They form a band as children usually do."

It was pretentious to call the empty place a playground. On the ruins, wild vegetation formed a bush in the middle of the district. For the children, it was heaven. They observed the planes flying overhead. It was so exciting! The planes arrived in rows and the children admired the giant iron birds.

In the last days, the number of children increased. The playground was in the direct line with the final approach to Tempelhof airport. The children were waiting for the little snowballs falling from the planes. The snowballs were small parachutes, holding chocolates and candies. Rapidly, the children got used to the godsend. They chased and hunted the candies. They were not able to hold back their enthusiasm. They caught what they were able to and ran home with their prizes.

In the garden, Gerd, Trudi, and Esther heard the voices of children. Agitation, excitement, and happiness echoed in their shouting. They ran breathless into the garden, their faces red and their shirts wet from perspiration.

"Mammy! Mammy! Look what I caught today! Chocolate!" Little Fritz was the first to run to them with a small, white bag in the palm of his hand. He never had a chocolate bar before. The others followed him; their hands full of candy. It was a successful day for the Eberhardt family.

"See, what we have from the Americans!" Anna handed over her prize to Gerd.

He took the precious item into his hand. Gerd was astonished. What a kind of Army is this that allows carrying out such personal action? Trudi looked at the treasures and her face became white. *How the world can change in a few years!* She remembered the winter 1945, the high bombings. The enemies of yesterday, the friends of today...

Esther was happy and satisfied. She is on the right side with the right people, and John is awe-inspiring. She was impatient to be with him once again.

Chapter 20
The Coal Cargo

John sat in the pilot seat for twenty minutes, with motors running, waiting in line for the green light on the runway to take off in the direction of Berlin.

"It's 4:30 A.M. and already bad weather... If we cannot get away from here soon, we will not be able to start," he said anxiously.

"We can fly in even thicker fog than this, I think," remarked Garry, the radioman.

"Yes, we can fly," answered the second pilot, Josh, "But we cannot start though. The GCA navigation unit is thirty miles away from the runway. After takeoff, we have to reach a minimum altitude to receive navigation guidance from them. Without visibility, we might as well give up hope of ever seeing our mother again."

Seeing Garry's pale face, Josh began to laugh.

"Do not worry! We have a former fighter pilot at the wheel!" He tapped on Garry's shoulder. At that moment, the light changed to green and their attention turned towards the task.

Behind them, in the belly of the machine, there was ten tons of precious coal. Coal is difficult to transport by plane because the light coal dust sifts out from the sacks and seeps into the inner fuselage. This flight would be quite an experience for John and his crew. They were all exhausted. In the last days, they flew eight hours. Between flights, they spent around eight hours on ground duty. They had to land, park, shut off engines, and head for the snack bar. They had to walk over to Operations to obtain their return clearance. If they were lucky, they would sleep six or seven hours. The weather was changing. They ran into rain, fog, hail, and even snow flurries, all on one flight. The one-hundred-minute flight to Berlin was as usual; wind, holes and clouds. They saw Soviet fighters along the corridor. John and his crew got used to them. Today, they stood aside.

The hastily hired German personnel loaded the coal into GI duffel bags available now. Berlin was not able to wait for the arrival of cloth and paper bags. John's attention turned toward the altimeter. The coal, like a sponge, soaked up the humid air, and its weight increased. John felt on his hands that the plane was becoming heavier. He had to maintain an altitude of four thousand feet.

"We have to lighten the plane, guys!"

"What is the problem?"

"The humidity makes the coal heavier. We will not be able to land. The landing gear will not support that weight."

"What we will do?" The crew worried about the situation. John considered the possibilities.

"You will go aft and toss out some duffel bags of coal. We will lighten the plane as we would lighten a ship."

Josh and Chuck spent the next fifteen minutes tossing out the precious coal. They were frozen. The coal on their hands and their face gave them a wild appearance. They longed to arrive in Berlin.

Over Berlin, they had to spend more than a half an hour waiting for landing permission. The final approach at Tempelhof was between residential high-rise buildings. John had the impression he was landing on the streets of Berlin. The wings were almost touching the windows. John had to be precise. He excelled in precision.

The plane taxied to its loading place. An MP officer approached their plane.

"Lieutenant John Carpenter?"

"Yes."

"Please come with me. The Commander is asking for you."

They went with quick steps to the main office. Colonel Howley, the military Commander of West Berlin awaited him.

"Lieutenant, we need to haul coal to Berlin."

"Yes, Colonel. I just arrived with a full load."

"I know. Your cargo was ten tons. We need two thousand tons per day. That is the minimum and that's just for summertime. We will need much more than that in wintertime. In that respect, we have to build up reserves for the winter. We think it would be possible to drop entire coal cargos in Berlin. I want you to take a plane and try to find sport places or parks, where we would be able to carry out this operation."

"Yes, Sir!"

"Try it right away! There are your orders."

John spent hours flying over Berlin looking for a suitable place to drop coal in burlap bags from low-flying bombers. They tried the Olympia Stadium and the parks in Grunewald and Tegel without success. They were too small of a target, or too close to the Soviet sector or difficult to fly over them. When they tried to drop the coal, it smashed into dust, repeatedly. It would not be possible.

Colonel Howley took a deep breath. They had to increase the tonnage and fast. They needed more aircraft. Washington ordered General Clay to report to the Congress. He was on his way to Washington.

Colonel Howley contemplated the crowded airport. He marveled at the aircraft coming down skillfully through the bomb-shattered buildings around the airport. As the planes touched down and bags of flour began to spill out from their bellies, he realized that this was the beginning of something wonderful, a way to crack the blockade. It was the most beautiful thing he had ever seen. The personnel, American, Germans and British, with the same understanding as Colonel Howley, were convinced they would succeed. Everything was possible with their outgoing confidence, their strong beliefs and can-do attitude. *Will the politicians agree?* General Clay had a most important battle to win once again far from the battlefield.

Chapter 21
The Dealer

With curiosity, Bob Howard walked onto Alexander Platz, in the Soviet sector. He rode into the area in a jeep full of German journalists; they wanted to write a story on the situation beyond Brandenburg Gate. The camera around his neck and the pencil behind his ear designated him from afar as an easy mark. The black marketers knew his type.

"Mister, one hundred Marks for a carton of cigarettes..." whispered one of them.

"One hundred ten... Good Marks, Mister, Ami Marks..." and he put five twenty D-Mark notes under Bob's nose.

"You are coming to us from a different world. We still live here under the power of the cigarettes. Even the currency reform did not liberate us from its control. One-twenty? I pay one-sixty... one-seventy-five? Do you have coffee instead of cigarettes?"

Bob wanted to end with the discussion; the marketer did not give up though.

"I have also cuckoo Marks..."

"What?" Bob's interest was picked. He had the feeling he was hearing something new.

"Yes, the cuckoo Mark, you know, the Soviet Mark with the adhesive coupon on it. We do not know why they call it adhesive for it always falls off. They did not even have the correct glue."

Bob was about to laugh and it took great energy to maintain his composure.

"*Nein,* I do not want anything!"

"Oh, Mister, you have everything there, in the Western sectors — lipsticks, tires, vegetables, and fruits..." His voice became dreamy as he imagined all these fantastic treasures.

"And here? What do you have here?" asked Bob.

"Here? We have nothing. From where? The Soviets have nothing. They have newspapers and pamphlets, period. Those who still have a private enterprise receive no credit from them. In practice, that is the nationalization. We are happy, if we do not hunger. We are waiting with caution."

"What are you waiting for? What do you mean by 'with caution'? Do you still believe that the Western powers will leave Berlin?"

"Ah, no more... Not even the S-P..."

"What S-P?"

"Scholars in Prognosis. They are those, who until now heard the grass growing and were always on the phone with Stalin. What we are waiting for depends on S-M."

"S-M?" asked Bob. The man succeeded to disorient him.

"Yes, Sire Majesty S-M, alias the Soviet Mark against the Ami Mark, the D-M... We all are hanging on the Ami Mark. Here, in the Eastern zone the Soviets forbid it. The Soviets will punish those, who have it. Everything is different in the Western sectors. Do you hear it?" he said, looking to the sky. "Airplanes! All day and night, one after the other... They bombard us with chocolates and candies!"

For a moment, in silence they watched the sky and the long line of airplanes.

"We have S-M and D-M and change in coins. The Soviets verify the notes; they do not verify the coins though. The best way is to use them on the street. You will see if you take the streetcar, there, toward the Soviet Union, to Potsdamer Platz."

Bob separated himself from his journalist friends and tried to venture out on his own. He took the streetcar. Now, this was a financial adventure. He wanted to pay the fare. The conductor did not accept his coins. Bob would be able to use these for purchase of other merchandise such as food. No newspapers or fares though, those, he had to pay with the Soviet Mark.

"Why?"

"The headquarters of the streetcar company is in the Eastern sector."

"And when I live in the Western sector?"

Bob's question generated a lengthy discussion among the passengers. Everybody wanted to explain to him in detail.

"At first, you have to change sixty Marks into Soviet money, in Karlshorst. You know, that is the Kremlin of Berlin. Secondly, all enterprises in the Western sectors pay salaries partially in the Soviet Mark. All Berliners have both currencies in their pockets. The conductors, however, do accept new D-M coins."

The conductors of the international streetcar, those cars circulating West to East and back, were condemned to a slow death before the currency reform. For a while, they were making a fortune, taking D-M coins along the entire road in the Western sector and, before arriving to the sectors' boundary, changing everything into Soviet money with friends waiting for them. The godsend fortune did not last for long. In the Western sector, there are now buses for the Western inhabitants. The Soviets are already organizing a real frontier. The passengers have to change streetcars at Potsdamer Platz and undergo customs checks, and Eastern police officers verify their identity papers and passports.

Bob got out and looked around the frontier land of Potsdamer Platz. The shops' windows were without lighting and for the most part, empty. When merchandise showed up, Bob saw the announcement: *For display only.*

He met with his German friends at Potsdamer Platz. They exchanged their impressions. For months, Berliners heard the menace of the Communist press about the terrible fate waiting anti-Soviets after the withdrawal of the Allied Forces. Fear of the Soviets was greater than that of the Gestapo some years ago. The intimidation did not work, not any more. The airlift, which the Berliners heard night and day, was proof of the Western presence. The flow of vital supplies strengthened the increasing trust. The parade in the sky showed that the Allied Forces were able to carry out titanic operations with strength.

All of a sudden, panic rushed over the crowd. People were running in all directions, disappearing under the porches of buildings. Some of them were jumping on moving streetcars, endangering their lives. Cars drove faster. After a moment of hesitation, Bob and his friends understood the reason of the riot.

Twenty police officers arrived from nowhere. They stopped the people; they grabbed suits and coats, searched pockets, wallets, handbags, and stopped cars.

"This is the Soviet D-M raid," whispered one of the people to Bob. "Now they are here every two hours on a regular basis. Two Communist inspectors lead them in person."

Bob and his journalist friends tried to escape. They were not quick enough. When they presented their journalist passes, the police officers were even harsher. Before understanding anything, Bob and his friends found themselves in jail. They tried to maintain their composure and dignity not showing any sign of fear. In their hearts, however, insecurity overtook them.

Chapter 22
The Candy Bomber

Lieutenant Gal Halvorsen arrived from Alabama only six weeks ago. When he received his deployment orders, he had barely enough time before reporting, to park his car under a tree and hide the keys. Immediately upon arriving at the base, he found himself flying to Berlin with vital supplies. Now he hurried to his commanding officer. He had a premonition that he would receive a punishment for lack of discipline. He decided to take it with dignity. In his mind, he still saw the bunch of children in Berlin some days ago.

After two weeks flying with his squadron, he succeeded in getting permission for a personal trip to Berlin. He only wanted to get a picture inside the barbed wire. Kids, eight to fourteen years old came up to speak with the American pilot in uniform. The Lieutenant spoke poor German; the children spoke equally poor English. They met half-way and managed to understand each other. Gal Halvorsen felt struck how different these kids were. He participated on the North African and Italian campaigns during World War II and experienced the children begging for candies, gum and cigarettes. On the contrary, these kids here in Berlin were mature and had a clear understanding of what was important.

"Did you have flour? How many sacks of it?"

"Will you fly also tomorrow?"

The young children fast changed the conversation from flour to the subject of freedom.

"Someday, we will have enough to eat. Do not give up on us when the weather gets bad!"

"If we lose our freedom, we may never get it back."

This conversation impressed the Lieutenant and he took it at heart. He promised them, to return with chewing gum and chocolates dropped in tiny parachutes. He bought all the candies he was able to find and prepared the tiny parachutes from handkerchiefs. When the handkerchiefs were not enough, he used old shirts, GI sheets, and old shorts. He dropped these tiny parachutes, as he promised, at the landing in Tempelhof. He did not request any authorization for that. He assumed that the Colonel ordered him to the office for explanation.

"Lieutenant, you have mail and packages!" A navigator from the squadron stopped him. "I will help you with it, if you want."

"Help, you say... we shall see..." Gal Halvorsen did not understand. He had no time for conversation now, though. He entered the commander's office.

The secretary had the most beautiful smile on her face. "Oh, Lieutenant, I will help you answering your mail if you need help. Please, enter. The Colonel awaits you."

Gal Halvorsen was confused. Why did everybody want to help him? He took a deep breath and entered the office. The Colonel had a serious expression on his face.

"Lieutenant! What is this?"

The Colonel pulled out a newspaper with a photo on the front page, of an airplane with tiny parachutes falling from it. The Lieutenant nodded and tried to explain.

"You hit a journalist on the head with a candy bar and he spread this story all over the world! The general read it and called me to find out what was going on. I did not know anything about it! This will jeopardize my promotion! Why did you not tell me?"

"I did not think you would approve it, sir."

"You are right!" affirmed the Colonel. "The General, though thinks, it is a good idea. Keep doing it!"

Lieutenant Gal Halvorsen was relieved. It was important for him to pursue his action. He felt obligated to the children.

"Yes, sir!"

He was already at the doorstep, when the Colonel stopped him.

"Lieutenant, wait a minute!"

The Colonel opened the drawer of his desk and took out a carton of candy.

"Take this one with you." He threw the carton over the office to the Lieutenant. Gal Halvorsen caught it, smiling.

"Yes, sir!"

With the carton under his arm, he went to the mailroom. The personnel saluted him, warmly. "That is your mail!"

Halvorsen was stupefied. That was not one letter; it was a bag with hundreds of them!

"Those are your packages too."

Packages — a box of them! Now, he began to understand what all these proposals of help meant! The story went out and people in America became passionate about it. They wanted to help him and supported his action with their own enthusiasm.

His friends were waiting in his quarters. They were ready to bombard Berlin with candies! His renegade idea became an operation. The American Confectioner Association asked how much candy and gum he would be able to use. Twenty-two schools in Chicopee Massachusetts converted an old fire station into a local headquarters. They made the parachutes, tied on the candy or gum and sent him the finished product. The entire squadron airdropped the candy over the city of Berlin to the eagerly waiting children.

They did not yet know that in the coming months they would airdrop two hundred and fifty thousand tiny parachutes over Berlin. They received so much candy from the American people that they were able to send it also to children in schools and hospitals. The most beautiful, spontaneous initiative of the airlift had begun right then.

Chapter 23
The Cannon

John was at the final approach of the Rhein-Main base. Today, this was his third flight from Berlin. He was tired because this last flight had been especially difficult. The autumn weather is always unpredictable; he knew it from his experience in the last few years. Germany is one of the most difficult weather forecasting areas in the world. During the winter, the meeting of nearby warm Gulf Stream with the cold North Sea generates a mixture of broadly varying temperature and humidity. Accurate forecasting became a major problem.

John trusted the weather forecast he received. The B-29 squadron in England had the assignment of continuous weather observations. Another B-17 squadron, operating from Wiesbaden, reported on flight conditions in the airlift corridors every twenty minutes. The pilots ahead reported every weather condition and the forecasting team used their reports extensively. John knew though that a change of one degree in temperature or a few knots change in wind force would generate a variation of visibility making the difference between a successful landing and heading back to the base without landing.

At takeoff, the Soviets directed a searchlight to the cockpit and blinded him for a minute. The crews became accustomed to that harassment. The Soviets did not miss a night without that exercise. At the halfway point on the route, they flew into a thunderstorm. The aircraft went from two thousand to eight thousand feet altitude and back again. The cockpit was dark, and then lightning struck around them, turning the plane brighter than daylight. The air corridor was twenty miles wide. That was enough to fly with the big four-engine Skymaster. There was no possibility, though, to divert from the route in case of bad weather such as this thunderstorm. John and his crew were relieved when they landed.

After the long hours of duty, their single wish was a good night's sleep. This night, however, the pilots had a matter to settle with the Army Administration.

The Army and the Air Force shared the Rhein-Main base. When the pilots on night duty would have gotten to sleep for a short time, at 6:00 A.M. a cannon would go off to announce reveille for the Army troops.

John participated on several meetings with the post commander. They tried to come to an agreement. The airlift ran on the long term. The crews flew in three shifts permanently. They needed appropriate rest. It was difficult enough to sleep without window coverings. The cannon shot every morning, in the moment when the crews just got a rest, generated an overall turmoil among them. The pilots decided to take action on that symbolic vestige of West Point.

John rushed to the warehouse. In that late hour, the sergeant was not there. A new recruit, a young private stayed at the desk.

"I need rope, one hundred feet," said John, calmly.

"What is this? You are the third pilot tonight asking me for one hundred feet of rope. What do you need it for?"

"If we miss the runway at the landing and finish in the mud, we pull out the plane from the sludge with it!"

"You pull it out?" The young private stood with open mouth, in disbelief. John needed all his self-control to not begin to laugh. The joke worked to perfection.

"Of course. We, peasants, are using peasants methods."

"What peasants?" The astonishment of the young private was complete.

"Yes. We are hauling potatoes, flour, coal, and milk in our flying trucks. We are peasants of the sky! Didn't you hear?"

"Sure, sure." whispered the boy, and gave the rope to John. Chuck and Gary waited for him outside the warehouse. When they heard his joke, they left the premises, unable to hide their amusement. They took the ropes and rushed to their quarters. The other pilots and crewmembers were already set up. The action planned for this night excited them.

The young, stubborn men left their quarters and approached the cannon area. No guard was present. Under cover of the night, they encircled the cannon. In silence, they pulled it behind the four-story barracks next to it. Four of them climbed the building and were already on the top of it with blocks and tackle. It took them another twenty minutes to haul the cannon to the top of the building. With strict military discipline, they worked in silence according to the plan they worked out in the last few days.

The action was carried out with success and left them satisfied. The celebration was complete in their quarters. No one would fire that cannon at 6:00 in the morning, any more!

Chapter 24
In Jail

"What we are doing here?" Bob asked his journalist friends. "How did we end up in jail?"

From Potsdamer Platz, the cops transported them to the sheriff's office and after confiscating all their equipment, they found themselves in the ward with others arrested at the same time. The ward was a sinister place; gray, uncomfortable, scary. Bob did not understand the situation. *Whose orders are these police officers carrying out?*

"At first, you have to understand that we have two police organizations in Berlin. The Markgraf police are the subject of Soviet supervision."

"Why Markgraf police?"

"Markgraf is the name of the superintendent. The Soviets nominated him. He has high recommendation from Moscow. The police officers are all fervent communists. Markgraf nominated a gardener as his second. By all evidence, the gardener also received high praise from Moscow!"

"All these officers are well armed, I noticed," said Bob, and tried to obtain more information from his inmates.

"Of course, they are armed to the teeth!"

Bob turned to his journalist friends.

"Did you hear that? There are international agreements to avoid the remilitarization of Germany! Without democratic structure and civil supervision, they have no right to create German armed forces!"

His friends were smiling.

"When are the Soviets burdened with any agreements? They consider only their own interests!"

Bob wanted to learn more about the people around him.

"Why are you here?" he asked a man in his forties, who was standing in a corner and sweating in his raincoat.

"I had 25 D-Marks in my pocket. The possession of D-Mark is forbidden in East Germany and thus it is also forbidden in East Berlin."

Bob turned to a young man with hands in his pockets.

"What happened to you?"

"I was reading the *Daily News*. That is a newspaper financed by the Americans and thus forbidden in Eastern Berlin. The possession of a non-authorized newspaper is a crime. Every day we have less freedom."

"I assume you are American, an American journalist?" someone asked Bob. The man with gray hair had a serious expression.

"Yes, I am..."

"Thank you. As long as we hear the noise of the planes over our head, we know that hope is not lost." The man grabbed Bob's hand for a warm handshake.

The guards interrupted Bob's investigation. They must lead the journalists to a small office-like room in the rear of the building. A table and four chairs were the only furniture. It was better than the cell. Apparently, the guards wanted to separate them from the others to avoid any further communication.

Bob was upset. He has rights! They do not have to treat him that way. He began to wave his hands and he claimed a phone call. He wanted to communicate with his embassy. His efforts were unsuccessful. The guard pulled Bob's pencil and the notebook out of his hands and pushed him back against the wall where he became disoriented for a moment. That was enough for the guard to close the door on them.

"Calm down," the German journalists told him. "It is dangerous to be anti-Soviet nowadays in East Berlin. Several thousands civilians simply disappeared. Many of them were inhabitants of the Western sectors. General Clay had even drawn up a plan. In the case of an evacuation, at least twenty thousand Berliners have to be transported to West Germany in order to protect them from Soviet vengeance!"

"I cannot believe that!" Bob was upset.

"We are different, do not worry. We have American and British news passes. On the top of that, you are American. They know they are not able to harm us! They do not want complications. Wait for the moment!"

Patience was not Bob's best characteristic. The treatment without any democratic measure, despising all civil rights unnerved him. It hurt his sense of justice. His emotions were boiling.

The door opened and two guards arrived with plenty of German sauerkraut with sausages and a pitcher of water.

"Do you see? We told you! Now, they want to show us, how rich they are. That is the disinformation!"

They enjoyed the godsend of food. After the dehydrated potatoes, the journalists found the forgotten taste of sauerkraut marvelous. They tried to sleep, but were keyed-up and alert. Suddenly, they heard rushing steps and the key turned in the lock. A man appeared on the doorstep.

"Good evening! My name is Hans Stolzer. I will help you. Come with me!"

Hans Stolzer came to the police station with official papers and negotiated with the guard. They called Central to verify the information. When they received the green light, they released the journalists. The police officers handed them back their equipment including cameras and flashes. Hans Stolzer accompanied them to the car in the street. They did not say a word before getting in the car and rolling toward West Berlin.

"You are lucky!" said Hans Stolzer. "Yesterday, in Wannsee, the Military Police stopped a limousine for speeding. They took the passenger and the driver to the police station. Can you guess who the passenger was?"

The journalist awaited the answer with interest.

"Marshal Sokolovsky! The MP released him after the kind intervention of General Clay. All of Berlin is laughing at the story! I do not know if this incident helped you, however, the Soviet authorities were quick to handle your case at this time!"

The passengers in the car were laughing as the Berliners did. The news spread throughout Berlin at the speed of light.

"Next time, when you want to see *Don Giovanni* in the State Opera House, leave the American Dodge at the checkpoint and walk the last few blocks," added Hans Stolzer tapping on Bob's shoulder.

They were dead tired, however, relieved and satisfied. They passed the Brandenburg Gate and when they entered the American sector, they took a deep breath of freedom.

Chapter 25
The Doll

Trudi gently brushed the long hair of her daughter. Anna was excited about the day. Esther entered the kitchen and was not able to contain her admiration.

"Anna! How beautiful you are today!"

"I will go to the airport! I will see the planes and the pilots!"

"Is it true?" asked Esther, looking to Trudi.

"Yes, of course, we are all going there. We will take this opportunity offered by the U.S. Air Force to see these planes and pilots who are keeping us alive."

"You are right," said Esther. "The Air Force organized series of demonstration flights. I will help you!" The single idea of the program thrilled Esther.

When they arrived to Tempelhof Airport, they found the big gates wide opened. Berliners came by hundreds to approach their heroes.

The Commander of the U.S. Air Force, Curtis LeMay, ordered the open gate program aimed to celebrate the birthday of U.S. Air Force. The American Air Force had a history of forty-one years, but only one year ago that it became a separate strike force. General Curtis LeMay wanted to celebrate by establishing new records. Before the eyes of the enthusiastic onlookers, planes made uninterrupted missions between the airfields in West Germany and Berlin.

On the Tempelhof Airport in Berlin, Frank Howley, the Military Commandant of Berlin opened the celebration. "I consider the Airlift as the most beautiful expression of America's interpretation of democracy and readiness to help one's fellow human beings in need that I have ever seen" he said to the reporters.

The Eberhardt family, like all the other visitors, admired the Thunderbolt fighter planes as they demonstrated dangerous maneuvers. In her best dress, little Anna, was walking all around the airport. She had a flower bouquet. She intended the flowers for an American pilot. At the unloading zone, she was able to approach one. The American laughed and teased the girl, signaling his thanks to the family, with the flower bouquet.

John flew all the day. Despite the celebration, the pilots had to haul a record tonnage. At the Rhein-Main and Wiesbaden airports, thousands of Germans visited the hangars. The fire brigade simulated a plane crash to demonstrate their emergency procedures. The special appliance transforming salt water into drinking water attracted many onlookers.

The celebration attracted even more traders and marketers with various goods than usual. John was tired in the afternoon and upon finishing his duty, noticed a marketer selling toys. Children encircled him and looked with envy to the treasures that, for the most part, were out of their reach. The toys were much too expensive for their parents.

John noticed a little girl in a stroller. She discovered a doll among the toys. Overly excited, she motioned to her mother. The scene made John smile. He went to her mother and took the little girl out of the stroller. He talked with the trader, and bought the doll she wanted. The little girl was giddy with joy as her mother stood by astonished. That was the first doll her daughter ever received.

John was happy. It was an overwhelming feeling to make the little girl as happy. When he saw among the merchandise the elegantly fashioned wooden tennis racquet, he bought it at once. *I also merit having a toy,* he thought. He joined the crowd in the mess hall, where a giant cream cake waited the pilots. The commander of the airlift used a sword to cut the special cake. They also bit into some coal dust mixed with the cake filling.

The pilots realized the first big record of the airlift, in twenty-four hours, in six hundred and fifty-one flights, they hauled fifty-five hundred and five tons of coal to Berlin.

Chapter 26
In Washington, D.C.

General Clay stopped for a moment and looked upward to the majestic entry of the Capitol building in Washington D.C. Although he had plenty of time, his nervous energy urged him to hurry upstairs. He had to give a report on Germany, including all details of the Berlin Blockade, to Congress and to the National Security Council. He had to be convincing! He sat down in front of the senators with the certainty that his thorough knowledge of the subject, his enthusiasm, and strong belief would help him to obtain what he came for — airplanes and continued financial support.

"General Clay," The President of the Commission opened the session, "as you know, in the frame of the Economic Recovery Program, we budgeted roughly 16.5 billion dollars to bolster the recovery of Europe. We did it at a time when, in the postwar budget cuts, we virtually disarmed the Pentagon, and when numerous domestic agencies submitted claims for enlarged welfare programs. In addition, the financial efforts provided for Germany alone including the Berlin Airlift, are amounting to around one hundred forty-seven million dollars. We forecast another forty-three million dollars in the next budget period. Before coming to the special situation in Berlin, let me ask you, General, how Germany is doing, and what are the prospects for the German people."

"In the first place, I must inform you about the tremendous success of the currency reform." General Clay prepared his answer in advance. "Be it in the American, British, or French zone, the effects were evident — immediate increase in produce and merchandise. The offer of vegetables, fruit, and butter increased not only in quantity but also in quality. Bakeries even offered cakes and pies. Deliveries of milk are increasing constantly. For millions of Germans, the new D-Mark represents a new world and a new future.

"Industrial production increased in the same proportion," continued General Clay with pride. "The industrial output reached seventy percent of the 1936 level and is improving on a regular basis. The unemployment rate is decreasing from month to month. Of course, I admit, this evolution is and never will be rushed enough, taking into consideration the burden it represents to the American taxpayers."

Robert Murphy listened to the discourse of General Clay. The two men knew each other well. Robert Murphy acted as political advisor to the General and was on several diplomatic missions in Moscow. His point of view was valuable.

"Senators, we cannot have a clear view on the German situation without pointing out the disastrous economic situation in the Soviet zone of Germany. According to the original agreement between the four allied powers, we are trying to preserve and to rebuild the industrial equipment permitting the German nation to stand independently on their own feet. The Soviets, to the contrary, confiscated all what they could from plowshares to rollers and they transported them to the Soviet Union violating, by that fact, this international agreement." Robert Murphy knew his topic perfectly. "In the beginning, they dismantled full facilities to rebuild them in the Urals. In so doing, they damaged the machines and were not able to use them. Afterwards, they dragged out the workforce — technicians and specialized workers. This did not work either. Now, they have discovered the best solution for them, using the equipment and the workforce where they are. They entitled themselves to ninety percent of the production, which they export to the Soviet Union."

General Clay nodded. The reports he received underlined the spreading hunger in Eastern Germany.

"It is the same when it comes to food. The German population in the Soviet zone is starving due to the export of foodstuffs. In the last ten days, two hundred and fifty wagons per day left with four thousand two hundred tons of meat and fish, and seven thousand tons of sugar and marmalade. In the last year, they confiscated fourteen thousand tons of wheat and six thousand tons of barley."

The senators on the commission were sensitive to that point. Their attention increased. Many in political circles did not believe in the success of the airlift. Berlin is not defensible from the military point of view. It is impossible to maintain a large-scale airlift over the long run. Some politicians advocated evacuating the city, avoiding the embarrassment if the massive airlift did fail. They hoped to obtain the respect of international agreement regarding West Berlin by strengthening the economic counter-blockade. The president directed the investigation toward that crucial question.

"The facts presented by you will take us directly to that central question: as economic issues are important to the Soviet Union, would the counter-blockade alone be an efficient response to the Berlin blockade?"

"No. The subject is more than Berlin alone." General Clay radiated conviction around him. "We defend freedom in the world. We are already limited in the range of that freedom. All new detractions from it, as small as they might be, will let our opponents think that they would still be able to obtain further limitations. The Soviets want to drive us out of Berlin. If they succeed in that project, they will demand all of Germany."

Dean Acheson, the former assistant of the secretary of state, a graduate of Harvard Law School, believed in the politics of firmness in face of the Soviets. This was the appropriate moment for his intervention.

"We have to adopt a firm attitude against dictators," said Dean Acheson, strongly. "Let me quote Winston Churchill: *There is no security when we give to dictators what they want, be they national socialists or communists.* Staying in Berlin will prove to the Soviets our determination and our strength. Time will work for us. We are strong and the strong are able to wait."

Secretary of State General George Marshall remained silent up until that point, and then felt that at this moment, it was necessary for him to speak.

"We are in Berlin as a result of international agreements regarding the occupational zones in Germany and we have the intention of staying there. The attempt of the Soviet forces to block the civilian population of Berlin raises fundamental concerns. Our partners and allies follow us in that operation. Our allies are not able to support the financial effort for the blockade. They are not able to face the Soviets without us. Our strength and consistency will calm them and they will provide us with the necessary support."

General Clay felt relieved by the intervention of the Secretary of State. His support was decisive.

"According to our latest studies," he continued with a firm voice, "we are able to transport food and other vital supplies to Berlin via air in a greater tonnage than we first thought. We are ready and able to maintain this airlift as long as it is necessary and even during the coming wintertime. Therefore, the negotiators will have at their disposal the necessary time to conclude an agreement."

"Is there any internal resource to back this operation? How is the economic situation in Berlin? If there is a West German recovery, would it be possible to use their financial results to any extent?" asked the President of the Commission.

"It is difficult, I have to admit," confided General Clay. "The West German population support and help Berlin. They are motivated in that respect. The German Post Office will surtax each postal parcel in circulation in Germany. The result of around twenty million D-Mark will go to the City Magistrate of Berlin. We are making an important effort to maintain industrial activities in West Berlin. The jobless rate is high. The airlift is able to provide work for thousands, but it is not enough."

General Clay was particularly proud of the economic incentives implemented by his administration.

"We planned an advertising campaign for goods produced by companies in West Berlin and transported to West Germany by the airlift on the return flight. In that advertising campaign, we will label these products with a distinctive mark, a standing bear with a broken chain around the hip and an inscription in a circle: *Made in Berlin under Blockade.* We are also implementing a new program to provide interest-free loans to business enterprises. We have to maintain life in

Berlin, not just feed starving people. That will be our strength."

"General Clay, winter is coming. What is your solution for the coal deliveries? Is there any chance to overcome this difficulty?"

"There are coal deposits in Berlin," stated General Clay, "representing a possible production of five hundred tons per day. Geologists discovered its existence still before World War One. At that time, the specialists did not advocate the somewhat expensive exploitation of this mediocre thermal quality coal. That is true. From our point of view, even the partial recovery of the daily requirement is already a victory. We would forecast the opening of the industrial exploitation for next year."

General Clay took a deep breath.

"These coal deposits, thus, are not the complete solution for the coming winter. We need to transport coal in great quantities to Berlin. From a practical viewpoint, we need more planes in order to expand the airlift."

"This decision must come from the National Security Council. We have no authority to increase the budget. The Armed Forces, the Ministry of Defense, and the National Security Council are able to reorganize expenses and financial capacities at their disposal in order that operations be strengthened in Berlin," stated the President of the Commission, closing the session.

General Clay was disappointed. He hoped for a rapid decision and was eager to fly back to Berlin. He did not give up hope though. He would participate at the military meeting held at the National Security Council. He would fight until the end. *These aircraft are essential! Without them, the winter campaign will not succeed.*

In the National Security Council, U.S. Secretary of the Army, Kenneth C. Royall, examined the serious expression of General Clay. He too, realized that the situation was critical and peace was at stake.

"We succeeded in increasing the tonnage around four thousand tons per day with the current number of planes," began General Clay in his report. "The Royal Air Force provided the airlift with the Sunderland Hydroplane, the only plane capable of transporting salt.

They also provided tanker airplanes for the transport of fuel in large quantities. At this moment, we carry out the coal deliveries in sufficient volume. For the coming winter season, however, we must increase this tonnage."

Kenneth Royall cut straight to the chase. "What is the total number of planes you require, General?"

"We need a total of three hundred and fifty four planes at our disposal in order to maintain the current numbers and frequencies of flights." General Clay put the statistics report on the desk. He wanted to be as precise as possible. "The average daily number of Skymasters in service is one hundred and twenty-eight, which means eight to ten flying hours each day. This is the actual 'flying time' and does not include loading, unloading, or time for aircrew changes. These aircraft are making four to five trips a day, to and from Berlin."

"If you have one hundred and twenty-eight in service, where are the other one hundred and ninety six airplanes?" asked General Vandenberg. The Air Force Chief of Staff was puzzled.

"They are down for maintenance or spare parts," answered General Clay. "As you know, the Skymaster is a passenger plane. We modified it to haul cargo. This aircraft is carrying heavier loads than it's been designed for."

"We have also to add," said General Bradley nodding understandingly, "that cargo such as coal causes abnormal maintenance problems. With the coal dust entering even the fuselage, the aircraft will become heavier. I received reports indicating that some of the Skymasters arrived for complete check up, overweight by a thousand pounds because of the coal dust! We have also to account for engine failures, crashes and other unscheduled maintenance and repairs. For guaranteed success of the airlift, we definitely need more planes!"

General Hoyt Vandenberg was already aware of these problems. He justified his opposition to the sending of additional planes with another argument.

"An increased commitment in the Berlin airlift would seriously disrupt our other operations nationwide, and would also affect our worldwide operations!" General Vandenberg made his point clear. "Do not forget that in the event of armed hostilities, enemy bombers would destroy a large number of planes at the beginning of the armed conflict. This would negatively affect the U.S. ability to wage strategic warfare. We have to preserve our strike force!"

General Clay was ready with the answer.

"The Soviets are able to strengthen the Cold War. They are not, however, in a position to initiate a true armed conflict. They are painting the specter of war on the walls, but they will think twice before launching armed hostilities." The persuasion of General Clay heated up the atmosphere of the meeting. "Their tactic is to generate unrest and anxiety in order to provide a perfect environment to seed the grains of communism."

There was silence for a moment; the participants of the conference were deep in their own thoughts. General Clay broke the silence.

"I would still advocate forcing the blockade with an armed convoy. If the Soviets let us pass through, it is the end of the blockade!"

General Bradley became edgy at that.

"General, we have already examined this possibility." He said vehemently. "This is a war of nerves. Let us be cool-headed and concentrate on the airlift!"

"That is perfect with me," answered General Clay. "In that case, we need more planes!"

"You will also need a third airport! With two airports, you are not able to handle the number of flights you forecast! Without a new airport, it is not useful to send you more planes," stated General Vandenberg, who still did not give up his opposition to the additional planes.

William Draper became Army Under Secretary after being economic advisor of General Clay in Berlin. He was familiar with the volume of food and other supplies necessary to sustain Berlin. "General, there are already plans in that respect. Our French allies proposed a convenient site in their zone at Tegel."

William Draper decided to lend his full assistance to the cause. "I support General Clay to the fullest extent. We need more planes and we need to construct this new airport. Moreover, it will give jobs to thousands and thousands of Berliners and improve their economic situation."

General Albert Wedemeyer, Army Chief of Plans and Operations, listened to the debate. In his mind, other concerns took form. To succeed with a full-scale airlift, they would need an experienced leader. Wedemeyer was U.S. Army theater commander in China during World War II. The legendary "Over the Hump" airlift supplied him with seventy-one thousand tons of material to China. Even though all air traffic channeled over the sixteen thousand foot high Himalayan Mountains, the crews delivered a tonnage far beyond what any airlift carried before. General Tunner, the commander of the "Hump" Airlift, would be the perfect commander for this full-scale operation.

"You will need General Tunner to command the Berlin Airlift. This operation is and will be by far the most important airlift operation of our time," continued Wedemeyer.

"We are doing very well at present. We are already hauling over four thousand tons a day," answered General Clay. He needed airplanes and everybody here had advice, but no airplanes. His frustration was evident.

"Yes, of course," said General Wedemeyer. "This operation, however, will fail without an experienced leader. At this moment, the most experienced commander in that field is General Tunner. I strongly recommend his immediate appointment."

Royall felt relieved. An experienced commander would bolster the tonnage without increasing the number of planes. Everybody looked satisfied, with the exception of General Clay. Will he ever receive his additional planes?

When they left, Royall stopped General Clay.

"The President wants us to step into his office."

The two men took the direction of the Oval Office.

Truman awaited them patiently. He was calm and determined. He cabled to Stalin and received his answer. Once again, Truman was upset. The Generalissimo was evasive. It was impossible to receive a clear answer from him.

Truman already formed his opinion. The Soviets did not believe in the success of the airlift. In their opinion, it was a waste of time. Its outcome would be the collapse of the allied forces. They would have to wait, time was working for them. Truman had a different view. He wanted to prove to them the contrary. The victory of a massive airlift would give an overwhelming superiority to the United States.

Truman contemplated General Clay. According to the expression on his face, he did not get what he wanted to receive.

"I am afraid you are unhappy, General Clay."

"Yes, Mister President, I am. We need the additional airplanes. That is the price of success in the winter campaign."

The President smiled.

"I know. Do not be unhappy, General! You are going to have your airplanes! As you know, I already ordered a full-scale airlift. I guarantee you myself that we will put at your disposal all necessary means to allow you to succeed with that operation. We will show to this son-of-a-bitch, what is an air transport operation!"

Truman had an ironic smile on his face. He trusted Stalin to make another inconsiderate move. *Without his crazy moves we would not get a penny from Congress,* he thought.

When General Clay arrived in Berlin two telegrams awaited him on his desk. The nomination of General Tunner as Airlift Commander was one. The General will arrive to Wiesbaden in the coming days. The second telegram came straight from the Oval Office. Sixty-six Skymasters will arrive in Wiesbaden and Rhein-Main next week on presidential orders.

The airlift continues.

Chapter 27
The Smuggle

Dieter parked the car three blocks away from the apartment of Willi Schlange, who was the contact man inside of Tempelhof airfield. Dieter set up the organization some months ago and it worked out to be very profitable. The black market had strong connections to Gatow, the British airfield, and Dieter proposed building up their operations in Tempelhof on a similar plan. Dieter earned much respect from Gerhard Sturm for his efficiency.

Dieter, always on the alert, noticed a man at the corner leaning on the wall, smoking. *What is he waiting for?* The neighborhood was empty; at this time of the day, there was no traffic. He decided to turn at the following corner and make a detour to Willi's apartment. He was running late for their meeting.

"Hello, Dieter, where have you been?" asked Marianne Seil, Willi's fiancée, opening the door. She was an attractive young lady with a beautiful smile. Dieter was fond of her, and sorry that she was engaged to Willi.

"Hello, Marianne. I was being cautious. Where is Willi?"

"Right here, Dieter." Willi stepped in, with a cup of coffee in his hands. He greeted Dieter and the two men sat down at the table. Marianne served coffee to Dieter. Coffee was an obvious luxury, but they could afford it. They had steady delivery of all kinds of luxury items.

"I set up a meeting for you with Kenneth Bromberg. The American is in a position to provide sugar in good quantity. Tony Springler will provide the freight. Do you remember him? He was the truck driver I introduced you to last week."

"I remember. We can accept all deliveries and in any quantity. You have free hand to organize." Both men were satisfied. "I have one concern though, Willi. It is about this man."

"What man?"

"I saw a man three blocks away from here on the corner. There was no reason for him to be there. When I recall our last meetings, I remember always having seen someone at that spot. Perhaps, it was not the same person. The bottom line is, we have to be careful. Something just doesn't smell right here."

"Don't be silly," said Willi.

"Okay, Willi, just be careful. We want to build up steady operations at Tempelhof airfield. You could be the key contact there. Do not lose sight of that."

Dieter left and once again took a roundabout route before reaching his car. The corner was empty. *I am becoming paranoid,* he thought.

Dieter was not paranoid, he was right. The man at the corner was a police officer investigating black market fraud. It was no secret to anyone that the black market was building up a large network in the shadows of the airlift. Profits were enormous. Moreover, the counter-blockade declared by the allied forces began to bring results. The Eastern economies and the Soviets became interested in various materials and merchandise. New openings were coming to light every day.

When Dieter arrived at *Zum Schwarzen Wald*, Gerhard was already in deep negotiation with his guest from Düsseldorf, West Germany. Herbert Seifert was a distinguished member of the English-German Club. His influence was far-reaching and his political connections assured him many opportunities in the future.

"Gerhard, the most important commodity is steel. The Eastern economy will be hardest hit by the counter-blockade. The industrial materials and merchandising will produce much more profit and possibilities than you could dream of. You have a good organization. Put it to the task!"

"I agree, Herbert, but I am not hot on this issue. I do not see myself doing business with the Soviets."

"I understand your position, Gerhard. Let me tell you what; you will be surprised how corrupt these 'men of the people' are. They preach equality, they preach social justice for everyone, but when it comes to money, they are greedier and more eager to have it in their pockets then you could possibly imagine."

"I already thought about that. They have to pay very high prices for materials not readily available to them. We can drain their blood. Steel, did you say? Do they want steel? And what else?"

"General Clay drew up a list of 'protected' sensitive materials like generators, radio-transmitters and tools. They need motors and engines, rails for railroads, imported raw materials and even iron and coal. They will run short very soon in food supplies and even in cattle. Any commodity you can name, there is a market for it."

"Let me think about it, Herbert. I have a connection, that's true. I am building up a good organization in Halle, in the Soviet zone. It is possible..."

Gerhard accompanied his guest to the door and his attention turned toward his lieutenant. Dieter stayed out of the negotiations. He was more involved in day to day transactions; Gerhard led the strategy of the group. Dieter was a loyal lieutenant.

"Come on, Dieter, let's rack them up!" said Gerhard and went to the pool table. They began to play while Dieter reported on the overall situation.

"We now have twenty-five persons on post at the Gatow airfield. Our operations are growing at Tempelhof. We have control of the Müller coal company. We began to collect firewood which is the most complicated undertaking. In Steglitz and in Tegel, the police are vigilant."

"That is good, Dieter. We are on the right track. I would like you to focus more on the operations in Halle."

"Do you mean, Esther?"

"Yes, and perhaps even more. We have to build secure communications and connections. We have to be ready when the time is right."

"Consider it done," answered Dieter.

The young men focused on the game. The organization had more projects than they could handle. Their future looked bright.

Chapter 28
Ultimate Sacrifice

Tom Crawley was inspecting the main runway in Tempelhof. At the time of construction, the engineers did not anticipate intense traffic and heavy airplanes. The frequency of landings started at every eight minutes, than became every three minutes and soon it will be reduced to every minute. The airplanes were waiting in line in the sky just as cars at traffic lights.

Tom Crawley pushed back his beret and scratched his head. The concrete was in bad shape. Along the runway, around seventy persons with shovels awaited the landings. As soon as a plane landed, they repaired the holes and the damage to the concrete. Two hundred and fifty persons worked in three shifts, twenty-four hours a day, and seven days a week. Tom Crawley knew they were not able to maintain those repairs over a long time.

He was looking for Esther. She had changed her wardrobe in the last few weeks. Esther understood that her town dresses were not suitable outfit for the airport. She found a GI uniform for herself. It was twice her size, but she coordinated it with style. She tightened the pant waist with a belt and used the shirt as a jacket. She folded up the pants at mid-leg level. A long scarf around the neck fell to her knees and gave to the ensemble a feminine touch. She adorned the boots with turned-down socks and put on a beret on her golden hair, curling with rebelliousness on her shoulders. She was a remarkable figure in the airport.

Gesturing, Tom Crawley yelled "Esther, come here!"

They drove the military jeep over to the construction site of the new runway. Its completion would not ease the congestion at Tempelhof. On the contrary, the increased traffic would add new complications to the airport operations.

Crawley was upset. Once again, the aluminum and steel bars necessary to the foundation of the runway had not been separated.

"Esther, we have to make it understood to loading services that they need more control and increased precision on their end! Damn! We have limited personnel, space and time! They have to get organized!"

They arrived at the office and Esther handed over the new dispatches to the Major.

"This is great news!" said Tom Crawley. "We will have the new airport! It's now official! Esther, can you see it? The French proposed Tegel in their sector. Now, I am sure we will succeed!"

Esther understood the situation of Tempelhof and Gatow. The tonnages hauled were increasing every day; however, it had not yet reached the quantities needed for the upcoming winter. The decision concerning the construction of a new airport was the best news she had heard in the last few weeks.

"They want us to find material for the foundation. We will need sand, stone, and other raw materials. Contact the Mayor's Office and look into any possibilities of local deliveries. We have to inspect the Tegel site and request several thousand workers for the job."

Major Tom Crawley and Esther drove to headquarters to appraise operational needs for the new airport. When they were crossing Berlin, Esther looked at the surroundings.

"Major, can we use the rubble?" asked Esther.

"What rubble?"

"Berlin is full of rubble. The bombing three years ago transformed the town into ruins. Look around you! There are piles at every corner! Is it possible to use the rubble for the foundation?"

"Yes, that is possible! In that case, we need trucks to transport the rubble to the Tegel site."

When they arrived to headquarters, their plan was ready. General Ganeval, Military Commander of the French Sector of Berlin, was proud to participate in the airlift.

General Ganeval was in the company of Group Captain Noel Hyde from the Royal Air Force. As soon as Crawley arrived, they began to examine the plans on the wall. What an ambitious structure, especially in a city under siege! The construction involved the creation of a fifty-five hundred foot runway, six thousand twenty feet of taxiway, forty-four hundred feet of access road, and twenty-seven hundred and fifty feet of access railroad. In addition, they needed over one million square feet of paved area immediately in front of airport buildings to allow easy loading and unloading of aircraft. They listened intently to Major Tom Crawley. The suggested use of shattered brick debris from the destroyed buildings of Berlin, paved over with asphalt was a great idea.

"We won't have enough trucks at our disposal."

"We will request their delivery from West Germany." Tom Crawley already drew up plans in his mind. "We already have two giant C-82s in the Air Force in Wiesbaden and we are awaiting three more. That aircraft is transporting spare engines for the Skymasters in service. The C-82 is big enough to transport tractors, bulldozers, and trucks to Berlin. The new runway at Tempelhof will be strong enough to allow their landing."

Major Tom Crawley transmitted his overwhelming energy to General Ganeval and Captain Noel Hyde. The coming challenges excited all of them.

"What will we do about the asphalt? We do not have asphalt in Berlin," remarked Noel Hyde.

"We will transport it to Berlin, of course. Wait a minute..." Tom Crawley reviewed the plans and made a fast calculation. "Considering fifty-five gallon drums, we will need ten thousand of them. We already have experience in drum transportation, which we used for fuel. Thanks to the RAF," Tom Crawley nodded with recognition toward Noel Hyde, "we receive the fuel now by tanker planes of the RAF. We will use that experience for the delivery of asphalt. It will, though, be necessary to designate a field somewhere in the airport neighborhood to warehouse the empty drums."

"We have only three months for construction," worried General Ganeval.

"It's in the workforce. The more workers we have, the faster we will build." Tom Crawley had already made up his mind. "We will need between seventeen and nineteen thousand workers."

"That is an enormous number of people!" objected Noel Hyde.

"It is not impossible, though. The unemployment rate is high in Berlin. We will help many families by giving them a job for some months! We will even offer warm soup by the shift. I am sure we can count on Berliners. They will be present. This is about their freedom and they know that."

Noel Hyde turned his attention toward Tegel Airfield Construction Plans hanging on the wall.

"Do you know that is the longest runway ever constructed at this time? Gentlemen, we are making history!"

Tom Crawley and Esther drove back to Tempelhof. They did not speak in the jeep; they were deep in thoughts. They lived these days with enthusiasm and they felt proud to be part of this epic undertaking.

They were crossing the district of Friedenau, when they heard an unfamiliar noise from the sky. A C-47 was in major difficulty. The pilot had lost control of his aircraft. They could see, he was trying hard to resume control. The final approach was between residential buildings and the pilot desperately struggled to avoid them. Suddenly, a section of wing broke off and flew upwards. The plane spun upside down. It was going to land on its top.

The aircraft disappeared from their sight. Seconds later, they heard a big explosion. They felt the earth shaking and saw the flames. Tom Crawley changed direction and rushed to the scene of the crash. The plane was in flames in the middle of the street, in front of an apartment building. When they arrived, the fire brigade was already there. They tried to secure the site and save civilian lives. Both the pilot and co-pilot perished instantly.

Esther's first thought was of John. She felt her heart missing a beat on the possibility that John could be the victim of a crash. Tears flowed from her eyes. There were several incidents here in Berlin and on the airfields in West Germany. Esther witnessed a crash for the first time. She was not crying alone. The onlookers, women and children for the most part, were also crying. These young men gave their lives to supply them with food instead of bombs.

Esther could not sleep that night. Jumbled thoughts haunted her mind. She wanted John at her side; she wanted to know that he was safe. She could not wait to be in his arms again.

She avoided passing through Friedenau for some days. The memory of the crash was unbearable to her. When she must cross the street one week later, she wanted to turn her gaze in the opposite direction. All of a sudden, she noticed the beautiful flower bouquet and the stone memorial on the wall of the building. She stepped forward to see it.

We were once enemies, yet you gave your lives for us. Now, we are in double debt to you.

She stretched her hand and touched the stone. She caressed it for a moment. She felt inner peace in her soul. The Berliners will not forget. The two young men would stay in their memories for the times to come. *Only those are dead, who are forgotten,* she thought, touched in her heart. *Those young men are not dead any more.*

PART IV.

LIFE IN THE DARKNESS

Chapter 29
The Commander

The wind blew with force this afternoon. Here, in Northern Germany, the autumn and winter arrived fast. In the overall mist, the Celts discovered early-on the twenty-six hot mineral springs generating a mild climate. At the southern foot of the Taunus Mountains, they founded the first settlement along the Rhein River.

The small, time-resisting settlement became Wiesbaden, the capital of the local nobility. The former royal and ducal residences overlooked the picturesque downtown. The cure building with its casino suffered during the war, but the downtown conserved its feudal charm.

General William Tunner, after his landing on the Wiesbaden Air Base, did not contemplate, though, the old, charming Prussian downtown. The West Point soldier concentrated on his mission. He was one of the few persons who believed, in all honesty, that air transport would save Berlin. For the last few weeks, he had secretly hoped that he would receive his promotion to command this operation, humorously referred to as "LeMay Coal and Feed Company".

Who else could be considered for that mission? His outstanding success of the "Hump" airlift over the Himalayas qualified him for this commanding position. Air transport was his life. He was convinced and determined to lead the Berlin Airlift to the success.

He established his headquarters in an apartment building on Taunus Street, in front of a small park with hot sulfur baths. He lived with his closest associates in the Schwartzerbach Hotel, a block away from his headquarters. Most of his staff found home in the even closer Hotel Rose.

General Tunner took over as commander of the entire airlift. The Americans expended the most significant part of the financial and technical efforts including the personnel. The British agreement to place the RAF under American command gave General Tunner an overwhelming authority.

This morning, he was analyzing a map of Germany on the wall. The map indicated the exact location of the three air corridors: Frankfurt-Berlin, Bückeburg-Berlin and Hamburg-Berlin. The General remembered his first trip to Berlin some days earlier. In the southern corridor, used by the American planes from Rhein-Main and Wiesbaden, they had to fly at an altitude of five thousand feet to get over the Harz Mountains.

"Have a look at the map," pointed out the General. "The central corridor is shorter and in addition over flat terrain all the way."

"That is right, General," agreed Colonel Milton. "Considering this fact, the U.S. planes using it could make three trips for every two trips over the original route."

"There are bases all around," asked the General. "Where are they? Who commands them?"

"They are all British bases: Fassberg, Wunsdorf, Bückeburg, Fuhlsbüttel, Lübeck, Schleswig-Land, and we are equipping Celle," answered Group Captain Noel Hyde from the RAF. General Tunner turned toward Air Commodore Merer, the commander of the Royal Air Force and his second in command in the CALTF, the Combined Air Lift Task Force.

"Commodore, would the RAF authorize the U.S. Air Force to operate from British bases in Germany as well? As you can see, we would be able to increase the number of flights to Berlin."

"General, we want to succeed with the airlift by all means," answered Air Commodore Merer. "You have our cooperation. In Berlin, however, there are only two airports and their capacities will be the limitation for any increase in air traffic."

Group Captain Noel Hyde intervened at once. "I have just arrived from Berlin, Generals. The construction of the new airport at Tegel in the French sector is already in progress. The Berliners are showing up by the thousands to participate in that extraordinary construction. They are building the most ambitious airport design at this time with shovels and hand tools, as we have limited numbers of bulldozers and caterpillars available."

General Tunner smiled and observed the Captain, who was popular amongst the American officers. In contrast to the quiet reserved behavior of the British officers, Noel Hyde had an outgoing personality similar to that of the Americans. The Germans shot down his plane during World War II over Germany and he was captured. The Germans interned him in several prisoner-of-war camps. He earned his fame for always engineering escapes. General Tunner felt the enthusiasm of the British Captain. This was the attitude he needed for the success of the airlift.

"That is good news," said General Tunner. "We need to make a tour of inspection and I would include those British bases as well. Do you mind, Commodore?"

"On the contrary, General, I am pleased that you want to experience our sites for yourself. Group Captain Noel Hyde will be at your disposal."

This decision satisfied General Tunner. The team headed to the airport. When the car drove through the streets leading to the airfield, General Tunner remarked how pilots and crews were lounging around in snack bars. The General and his staff walked through the base, where a chaos reigned. The airlift operated without schedules. The loading and unloading lacked coordination, resulting in frequent delays. Pilots, crews, and ground personnel were all exhausted. They saluted the General with the hope in their eyes that a new organization would ease the pressure on their backs.

General Tunner made up his mind fast. While standing at the windows in the Operation Office of the Wiesbaden airfield, contemplating the congested airport, he gave his orders with a firm voice.

"As soon as a plane lands, a large truck with the unloading crew has to meet the aircraft at the ramp. From now on, the pilots must stand by their plane. An operations officer will meet them with the clearance slip and he will pass along any problems anticipated on the return flight. The weather officer has to provide information on the weather conditions directly to the pilots."

"General," intervened Colonel Ross Milton, "the pilots and crews have to eat as well!"

"You're right, Ross." General Tunner was smiling. Colonel Ross Milton commanded the first daylight raid on Berlin during the war some years ago. He always represented the best interests of the pilots in all discussions. General Tunner handpicked the officer for his staff for that very reason. "We have to implement a mobile snack bar to supply our pilots with coffee, doughnuts, hamburgers, and other sandwiches."

"Yes, Sir," said Colonel Milton "The pilots will be unhappy, General..." added Colonel Milton, hesitantly.

"Do not push too far, Ross! They are soldiers and this is a military organization after all!" reacted the General sharply.

"Wait a minute!" intervened Noel Hyde. "Would it be possible to hire attractive girls for the mobile snack bars? There is nothing more enjoyable than chatting up cute girls during the wait time!"

The senior officers turned toward him, and all of a sudden, he felt intimidated. "I would enjoy it... I mean..." he added sheepishly.

"You are right, Captain Hyde!" General Tunner smiled and gave the orders at once. "Ross, get in touch with the German Red Cross. They have to hire the prettiest girls in town!"

"We will assist in the tremendous increase in requests for marriage authorizations, General," added Ross Milton. "They will be sure to call us dating service."

The entire team laughed. As a matter of fact, the new procedures reduced the turnaround times by thirty minutes. General Tunner knew, however, further steps would be necessary to pass the difficult test of the wintertime.

Chapter 30
The Loft

"Mammy, me too, I want to go with you," little Fritz ran after Trudi and grabbed her skirt. The little boy did not want to miss the formidable adventure going on at that moment. Trudi and Esther went upstairs to look through the loft. They had not opened the loft at all for at least two years. The reason of this expedition was, however, not for cleaning up. Trudi hoped to find some treasure in the loft that she would be able to use in these days. Their life had taken an unexpected turn. They had electricity two hours during the day and two hours late at night. The coming winter would be freezing cold. Coal would be available for the inhabitants in limited quantities. The most part of it would go to the power station. An idea had struck Trudi some days earlier.

"Esther, we had a woodstove in the old days. Perhaps we still have it in the loft. It would be handy to use it now. We will be able to heat the kitchen and to cook at the same time. We will reduce our needs for coal or wood. What do you think?" Trudi enjoyed discussing every day issues with Esther, who was enthused about this project.

"Oh, Trudi, it will make me relive my childhood! We did not have electricity in our village. I will be able to help you. Cooking on a woodstove is special. I will show you how. Let us go at once! I am excited by this visit to the loft!"

The two women's project did not remain secret long and this adventure generated overall joy. When the door opened, the children burst through, making a path through dust and cobwebs. The loft looked to them as a forgotten pirate cave filled with treasures of the old world. While the children enjoyed the game of discovery, the two women were looking for the real treasure, which would give them the relief during the cold days ahead of them.

Where is the stove? Here it is! The stove stood in a corner, covered in thick dust, with all spare parts necessary for its use. They tried to move the heavy piece. Johann helped them, but the stove was still too heavy for them. All of a sudden, they heard voices from downstairs.

"Trudi! Children! Where are you?" Gerd arrived home from the hospital right then. To his astonishment, he heard unusual voices from the loft. When he learned the reason for the excitement, he agreed with the family. This old stove is a treasure for the wintertime. They spent the next hours moving the old piece downstairs and found a place for it in the kitchen. When the chore was finished, they were dusty and dirty and ash-covered and exhausted. The shadows of the afternoon turned up already, and they had a rest.

"By the way, Gerd, how it is possible that you are at home? Why are you not in the hospital?" asked Trudi.

"I am, to some extent, unemployed now." All eyes turned toward him.

"A surgeon? You cannot be unemployed!" whispered Esther.

"Yes, I can. We are not able to carry out any more surgery. Ether is highly flammable, and therefore, it is impossible to deliver it by air. We are now struggling with a severe shortage of ether. We have to save our supplies for emergencies."

"Oh, this is serious!" exclaimed Esther. "What will happen to the patients who need surgery that is not an emergency?"

"The military planes will transport them in hospitals in West Germany. They are already prepared to accept our patients if it would be necessary. The airlift will take care of that issue as well." Gerd, as the Berliners in general, felt admiration for these young pilots and for that military organization which protected their freedom and promised a better future for all of them.

"What happened to Herr Kupfer? The old man was sitting in the backyard and crying. I was used to see him smiling."

"Oh, that is sad, Gerd!" said Trudi, while explaining to him the shock of this morning. "We were awakened by a piercing lament that could come straight from the Old Testament. The scream came from the backyard. You know that the eighty-year-old Herr Kupfer maintained the little vegetable garden on the green field between the houses. The robbers ravaged his miserable garden during the night and took the pitiful lettuce, and potatoes. The old man with his white beard was trembling from the disappointment."

"That happened last year also. And the year before. Once a year, we experience this violation. That is a pity!"

"Yes, Gerd. Today, however, two potato beds mean Life in Berlin."

Trudi prepared some dehydrated mashed potatoes for the family. Little Fritz was not happy.

"Mammy, I do not want that. Everyday we have the same. I would like to have rice, and ham, and lettuce like Herr Kupfer." The little boy was almost crying.

"I know, my little Fritz. Be patient! One day we will have enough. By the way, Herr Kupfer has lost his garden. Eat your mashed potatoes and think about a freshly baked cake. You have an imagination, don't you?"

"The Schreibers have baked potatoes..."

"The Schreibers are communists. They are buying in the Soviet sector. We are not going there."

"Why?"

"Going to the Soviet sector is treachery. The Schreiber betray our freedom. We will stick to these dehydrated potatoes and dehydrated milk and the cold and the candles in spite of the electricity. We will stay free."

"What is free?"

The little boy was not ready to stop asking questions. Esther took over from Trudi.

"Free is that you can complain here about the mashed potatoes. You are free to think, what you want. You are free to speak, what you want. You are free to write, what you want. You are free to believe, what you want. You have the right to elect a government and a magistrate. That is the democracy. By the way Trudi, do you know what is in the news?"

"No, tell me!" Trudi was curious.

"Hans Stolzer called me at the airport. He invited me to participate in the election campaign! The elections will take place soon and there is a lot of work to do! I am excited about it! I did never participate in that kind of organization! That will be my first election."

"That is impressive, Esther!" Gerd intervened in the discussion. "You have to be careful though. I heard the Communists are trying to disorganize the elections. I think these elections will, without doubt, split our capital in two parts."

The shadows were growing and they lit on the candles.

"What about your American pilot friend? How is he doing these days?" inquired Gerd.

"He is doing well. He will fly to Berlin during his leave. We will have some time to spend together."

"Oh, it's 6 P.M.!" Trudi looked up to the clock on the kitchen wall. "We have to run if we do not want to miss RIAS!"

The family left at once. Each evening, at this time, the loudspeaker cars from RIAS passed in the district. The neighborhood met on the playground, at the corner. Where children played in the afternoon, now adults were sitting on the rubble. While waiting for the information, they exchanged their experiences of the day and their political views, strengthening each other's spirit. Their attention was directed to the loudspeaker car that appeared at the corner. People recognized the voice of their favorite female announcer. This voice was more serious today than normal.

"On Monday, shortly after takeoff from Wunsdorf in the British zone, an airplane 'York' crashed, and four British airmen died in the accident. 'York' hauled eight tons of food to Berlin. The Americans had already lost nine crewmembers. Despite the losses, the airlift continues."

The people had tears in the eyes. The pilots and crews were dear to their hearts.

"We are able to maintain the Airlift to Berlin for as long as it will be necessary," declared General Clay to journalists. "According to Associated Press, in the last twenty-four hours the airlift brought in six hundred and seventy-five tons of foods alone beside coal and various goods in seven hundred and eighty-four flights."

Berliners were waiting for the information on the food distribution plan.

"The administration organized the following food distribution over the next days. In the Western sectors all cardholders are allotted one hundred grams of chocolate or one hundred grams of sugar on the special coupon #O this month. With meat coupons, the cardholders will receive fifty percent of their allotment in canned meat and fifty percent in egg powder in the first ten days, and frozen beef and pork in the second ten days. The administration will distribute twenty percent of the butter and eighty percent of the lard or margarine in the first and third periods, and forty percent of the butter and sixty percent of the lard and margarine in the second period. In the sector Mitte, one pound of onion on the coupons, E/F. In the sector Neukölln and Steglitz, 62.5 grams of dried fruits on the coupons #1 and #2. In French sector, around 125 grams of candles against coupon #74."

Some of the onlookers noted the information on paper.

"The magistracy of Berlin decided to purchase dried fruits in West Germany for the production of marmalade. The military commandants of West Berlin ordered the delivery of five hundred tons of coal for the hospitals in the Western sectors."

Besides the food distribution, the most important information concerned the electricity supply. It influenced the rhythm of their everyday lives.

"The BEWAG planned the following electricity supply program:
Group A and E
from 9 A.M. to 11 A.M. and from 8 P.M. to 10 P.M.
Group B and F
from 12 A.M. to 2 P.M. and from 10 P.M. to 12 P.M.
Group C and G
from 1 A.M. to 3 A.M. and from 4 P.M. to 6 P.M.
Group D and H
from 3 A.M. to 5 A.M. and from 6 P.M. to 8 P.M."

The RIAS always answered the communist propaganda. The onlookers waited the every day caricature with curiosity.

"The Soviet Administration promised sixty thousand tons of coal for the entire city of Berlin, Western sectors included. The Eastern sectors need fifty-seven thousand, two hundred tons of coal. The remaining two thousand, eight hundred tons will never cover the ninety-six thousand tons needed by West Berlin. Either the Soviet mathematicians or the Soviet intentions are wrong, or both of them. You are in luck! Imagine if the Americans were blocking Berlin and the Russians were running the airlift!"

A healthy laugh filled the air. The crowd took the path to their homes in a relaxed atmosphere. A couple with their little daughter stopped at Esther. They knew each other by sight without ever talking though.

"Good evening, Fraulein!"

"Good evening!"

"We know you are working on the American airport, in Tempelhof."

"Yes, I do. Can I be of help?"

"Yes, indeed. We read in the newspaper one week ago, that a pilot has two small children back home in Iowa. We would like to send them these presents as an expression of our gratitude for maintaining us alive and free."

Esther took the box in her hands. It was addressed to "Lt. Keller, Greenfield, Iowa". Unfolding the box, Esther saw two homemade rag dolls for Keller's children. The present touched her and she fought back her tears.

"I made it myself. Would you give them to the military authorities, please? Will they send them to the American children?" asked the little girl.

"Of course, darling." Esther embraced the little girl with warmth. "I will do it myself, first thing tomorrow morning!"

Chapter 31
Black Friday

This day began as a normal day in the life of the Berlin Airlift. The airports operated twenty-four hours per day; the rhythm of takeoffs was regular; in the air corridors, the uninterrupted line of the planes heading to Berlin was the typical crowd, the planes precisely three minute apart, and each of them flying at a speed of one hundred and eighty miles per hour.

General Tunner stood beside the Skymaster on the Wiesbaden airport. For today, he planned an inspection tour with his staff in Berlin. The staff organized different meetings in Berlin to coordinate the actions. Colonel Red Forman, personal pilot and good friend of General Tunner was at the command of the Skymaster. The weather was fair when they took off in Wiesbaden. They passed over the Fulda low-frequency beacon. The pilot made a 57-degree turn to enter the air corridor, where they disappeared in the clouds and became one of the countless small points on the radar screen of the operators on the ground.

In Berlin, on Tempelhof Airfield, Major Crawley worried about the day. They had sprinkles through the night and the runway was slippery. The apartment buildings surrounding the Tempelhof airport were hiding in thick clouds this morning. At this time of the day, the sprinkle grew into a rainstorm. In the tower, Major Crawley and the ground operations officer were not able to see the runway. They were not alone. The radars were not able to penetrate the sheets of rain either. The operators in front of their screen were nervous. The incoming Skymaster without sufficient visibility landed too far and the plane ran off the runway. Major Crawley left at once the tower to join up with the rescue team.

The aircraft crashed into a ditch at the end of the field and caught fire. By miracle, the crew escaped from the plane just before the explosion. When Major Crawley arrived, the rescue team already on site was struggling to extinguish the fire. The plane transported asphalt for the construction of the Tegel airport. The rainstorm did not help the rescue team. The flammable asphalt was perfect nourishment for the flames. The crews were at the rescue truck under cover, still trembling. The rescue team tried to clear up the runway. Major Crawley had a bad premonition. He was looking to the sky hoping for some relief.

At that moment, he saw the other Skymaster coming out of the clouds. The pilot had difficulty in maintaining his plane in a direct line, and touched down too late. All of a sudden, the pilot saw the fire ahead on the runway. To avoid piling into the fire, he had to brake with all the force he had. The tires blew and the plane became uncontrollable. The iron monster glissaded at high speed directly to the fire.

The team at the end of the runway saw death approaching them. The everlasting cigar in the mouth of Major Crawley fell on the ground. The rescue team froze in their tracks, looking to the Skymaster slipping toward them. The second miracle of the day happened, when the plane slid on its side and was immobilized in the mud. They avoided the disaster. The rescue officer was ironical.

"Major, you see, we are well served. With one shot we have two flies."

Major Crawley pushed the pilots in the jeep and with them, he hurried to the Operations Office. He took the radio and screamed at the tower. "What are you doing, for God's sake? Divert the traffic! We are stuck here!"

Total confusion reigned in the tower. Major Crawley felt that both tower operators and ground-control approach operators lost control of the situation. Since planes arrived every three minutes, the third incoming airplane appeared over the housetops. Visibility was still zero. The pilot saw what seemed to be a runway and prepared to land. Major Crawley noticed the bad approach. He jumped out from the jeep. Running toward the landing aircraft, he began to signal the pilot with his hands, and shouting even though he couldn't be heard. "No! Go away! That is not a runway!"

Major Crawley was despaired. His action was hopeless. Not being able to see him, the pilot understood too late that he picked an auxiliary runway still under construction and his airplane slipped in the rubber base at the side of the runway and ground-looped.

Major Crawley threw his cigar and damned the day. He ran to the Operation Office in the tower. When he entered the office, he felt the confusion at once. The radar operators were speaking nervously, and on their screen, the number of the small moving points increased every three minutes. Planes were still arriving on schedule.

"What is the situation," he asked the Commanding Officer.

"That is terrible. We are now piling up the airplanes in the sky. We instructed the bases in Germany to stop departures. We are, however, not able to stop planes already routing to Berlin."

"Berlin Tower. This is Air Force 37, requesting authorization to land. We have General Tunner on board. Over." The radar operator went white. What was he to do now? The Commanding Officer and Major Crawley watched each other with despair.

"Reserve a space for the General. What do you have free?"

"I can reserve a space at eight thousand feet," said the radar operator.

"Give me the microphone!"

"Hello Air Force 37. This is the Operations Officer at Tempelhof. We have incidents on the ground. Continue circling at eight thousand feet and wait for our signal."

Colonel Forman, the Skymaster pilot, informed the General. "Sir, there are incidents on ground; we have to wait for authorization. Do you wish to identify yourself?"

"No. Let the people on the ground do their jobs. I hope it will not be long. Let me listen to the conversations. Give me a headphone!"

The General listened to the pilots calling in with nervousness in their voices.

"Tower, I am now at twelve thousand feet. What do you want me to do, for God's sake?"

"I am now on the top of the stack. How long will it take?" "I have been circling now for an hour!"

"Maintain your route. We are cleaning up the runway."

General Tunner and Colonel Forman watched each other with astonishment. What is happening on the ground?

The telephone rang in the main office of the tower.

"Major Crawley, we have an issue here," called a sergeant. "We have aircraft on the ground coming off the unloading line and now they are at the end of the taxiway. We have now a traffic jam building up. They are not authorized to take off."

"Of course, can't you see what's on the runway? Hold them on the loading area."

"Yes, Major. Planes are already waiting in line though."

"Wait a minute. I'm coming," he said anxiously. He turned toward the Operation Officer on duty. "Can't you do something?"

"Of course not! Why are you surprised? We are unable to authorize any takeoffs! We must avoid collisions!"

Major Crawley left the tower and ran to the planes. The situation was serious. At the same time, it was also a most shameful situation in front of the General in the middle of the stack. Crawley was looking to the sky, hoping for a solution. The weather has to clear up! In that rainstorm, maintenance teams on the runway are not able to work efficiently.

General Tunner continued to listen to the radio. The planes, like gray monsters in the shadows, were flying in circles over Berlin. The pilots filled the radio with chatter, calling in, in near panic to find out what was going on. General Tunner became agitated.

"Here I am, flying around in circles over their heads. That is damned embarrassing! The Commander of the Berlin Airlift is not able to get even himself into Berlin!"

His staff looked at the General in bewilderment. The General lost his temper on rare occasions. He took the microphone and identified himself.

"General Tunner speaking."

"Yes, General."

"In order to avert a disaster, tell everyone in the stack above and below me to go back home, then tell me when it is okay to land."

The radar operators cleared the sky in twenty minutes. Air Force 37 was able to land at last. The General and his staff rushed to the tower at once to find out what happened.

"General, the twenty mile-wide air corridors limit our ability to maneuver! The air corridors are over or near to Soviet airfields. In the case as today, when a plane for any reason is unable to land, the pilot has a radius of twenty miles to circle in. In addition, they are circling almost over the two Berlin airfields!"

The General was not satisfied with the explanation. He had already made his decision.

"From now on, every plane arriving over Berlin will receive one single pass at landing. If for any reason, the pilot is not able to bring his plane in, he will return to his home base in West Germany. This will avoid planes being stacked in that small twenty-mile radius over Berlin."

The decision was clear and masterful in its simplicity.

When General Tunner entered the radar operators' room, he understood at once the second problem of this "Black Friday." Young recruits were sitting in front of the screens. For the major part, this was their first deployment.

General Tunner, exuding leadership, gave his orders at once. "Well, at first, let me tell you that we had a slight sample of the difficult winter weather. Today, it was a simple rainstorm. Tomorrow, we will have thunderstorms, heavy snow, and ice and fog with zero visibility. We have to be prepared for that! From now on, all planes in the Berlin corridors will fly under instrument flight rules, at all times, regardless of weather. This procedure will allow us to build up the necessary experience for the difficult wintertime ahead of us!"

The immediate implementation of the orders increased the efficiency of the airlift. The system worked as a conveyor belt. Success came in sight for everyone.

Chapter 32
The Construction

Trudi woke up this morning at dawn. For months, she had been unable to find a job. The "Spider", the fabric factory of Berlin, shut down its operations and, as many other women in the neighborhood, she became jobless. Martha, her husband's cousin, was already in the kitchen.

Martha lived in Dresden, an important railroad center that was vital to the German army during the war. On the night of February 13, 1945, hundreds of British and Americans bombers released a firestorm on Dresden, killing one hundred and thirty-five thousand people and demolishing eighty percent of the city. The explosions produced so much heat that people died, boiled in the bunkers. Nothing was left in Dresden. She took the road to Berlin to find family members there. She never spoke about the terrible journey from Dresden to Berlin.

When she arrived in the Eberhardt mansion, Trudi took care of her at once. Still today, she was a reserved woman who did not speak much, only a few words on some occasion. The war and the events marked her for life.

This morning, she made a coffee. The coffee consisted of a pitcher of hot water and a half-tablespoon of coffee. The liquid was light brown and without any taste. She pointed to the chair when Trudi entered the kitchen, and poured her some coffee, smiling.

"Oh, Martha, thank you. How lucky that you had gas this morning! The pressure is low in general." She sipped some coffee. "This is good. We will have something in the stomach."

All of a sudden, Johann appeared on the doorstep. Trudi was astonished.

"What is it, Johann? What are you doing up at dawn? Today, you do not have school, you can sleep longer!"

"Oh, Mother, may I come with you today?"

"You are just a child!"

"I am fourteen! I heard they are accepting children of my age. I can hold a shovel. Mother, please, I know how important it is for us, for all of us. Without the new airport, we will not survive! I can do something about it."

Trudi had tears in her eyes. She embraced the young boy who understood what was important. Construction of the new airport in Tegel provided work for thousands. Trudi, Martha and other women from the neighborhood all worked on the construction site. The salary was mediocre, but they had warm soup and bread once in a day. That was a godsend in these days.

It was still dark when they left the house. The road to Tegel was an expedition. The administration limited the access of streetcars to certain specified hours in the day because of the lack of energy. The streetcar was full, and left people along the tracks. People had bruises all over their bodies during the ride to work. Today, Trudi, Martha and Johann were lucky — they found a seat. The Berliners began to talk at once, and had a large choice of topics to talk about — currency, the blockade, hunger, the airlift, and the communists. A man with a red nose remarked in his deep, alcohol-husky voice, that the Soviets ensure a much better distribution of schnapps than the Americans do. The women in the compartment were furious.

"Yes? Do they distribute more schnapps? They suspended the distribution of milk for the infants though! What a good exchange!"

"Schnapps, you said. They would better distribute more potatoes, or why not candy and chocolate like the Americans? With candy and chocolate we are able to do something!"

The man tightened his coat and scarf. He tried to mingle with the passengers. He gave up his tirade about the positive side of the communism.

A young man beside Trudi, reading a newspaper, did not say a word until now. He folded it and put in the pocket of his coat. "Funny, this is funny. The whole world is speaking about us as the heroic people of Berlin."

"What's so funny about that?" asked Trudi, perplexed.

"What is so funny is that once again we are heroic and we are not able to do anything about it. What is heroic about our not wanting to fall in the conditions of our brothers," and he pointed toward the Eastern sector. "Our main complaint is the continuous noise of the airplanes above us. They are the heroes!" The young man observed the sky through the window of the streetcar. The passengers agreed in silence.

When Trudi, Martha, and Johann changed cars at the zoo, their number increased. The crowd flowed to the large tract of land, where the anti-aircraft artillery of Hermann Göring trained. Trucks transported all of them to the construction site. Along with trucks transporting the workers, were long lines of trucks filled with rubble. Thousands and thousands of unskilled laborers waited in line to receive their hand tools and job assignments. They all knew the new airport could be their salvation, the way to break the blockade and safeguard their freedom. They were here for a small salary, and for the warm soup and bread. They were here for their freedom. Without their enthusiasm, without the strong belief in a better future, their decisiveness would not reach out during the days, weeks, and months. The newspapers of the world were right after all. They were the heroic people of Berlin.

A car stopped beside Trudi and she recognized General Lucius Clay. The General had a meeting here with the other military commanders. They wanted to inspect the construction, main issue for the future of the airlift.

Sir Robertson was already here. His tall figure was visible from far. As per the family history, his destiny was in the military. He was officer during World War I. After, he participated on a military expedition in Northwestern India. In World War II, he filled an important position on the general staff during the campaign in Ethiopia and Italy before his nomination as Military Governor for Germany. With a riding crop under the arm, he dragooned the Berliners. His instructions were short, clear and efficient.

The British Empire was built by men like him, thought General Clay, while observing his British counterpart.

"Oh, General Clay! Good morning! Construction is advancing satisfactorily, isn't it?"

"Oh, yes, Sir Robertson. I agree."

The two men arrived at the mobile headquarter and greeted General Koenig in company of Brigadier General Jean Ganeval, military commander of the French sector of Berlin. The French were content to have an active role now in the airlift. Their government in France adopted a moderate position, but the French personnel in Berlin were carried away in the overall enthusiasm. The Americans built the airport; the French provided maintenance and loading personnel. They would be part of that big adventure at last.

"I want to inform you," began General Clay, "that we received several large C-74 'Globemasters' and giant C-82 'Fairchild Flying Boxcars' in order to be able to increase our airlift capacities. These huge airplanes are important to that construction. We will be able to transport large material and needed construction equipment to Berlin."

"Does it mean that we will be able to receive steamrollers large enough to flatten and compress the runway surface?" inquired Sir Robertson, showing increasing interest.

"Yes, it will be possible. However, the steamrollers are so large that even these giant aircraft will not be able to carry them. We will cut it up with acetylene torches at Rhein-Main before loading them for the trip to Berlin."

"According to my understanding," responded Sir Robertson, "we will have to provide necessary equipment to weld it together again in Berlin."

"That is right!" nodded General Clay.

"We will organize it. No problem!" intervened Brigadier General Jean Ganeval, in his strong French accent. "What is your standpoint concerning the two Radio Towers of the Soviet controlled Radio Berlin? The two towers, two hundred and forty and three hundred feet high, stick up into the forecasted approach path."

"Jean, don't you think, it is too early to worry about it?" inquired General Koenig.

"I do not think, Pierre." The two Frenchmen had different views on the question. They would not be French otherwise.

"I agree with Brigadier General Ganeval," said General Clay. "That will be a major issue when we will begin the operation of Tegel. We have to convince the Soviets to move them before that. We cannot begin soon enough considering the stubbornness of the Soviets."

"What? Do you want to convince them?"

Jean Ganeval became restless. In the resistance, he learned that in the decisive moment it is necessary to act immediately. In a military question, such a discussion had no place.

"I do not believe we will be able to convince them. You experience continuous harassments in the air corridors; do you think they will dismantle the towers because it's just the right thing to do?"

The British and the American generals breathed deeply. Oh, these French! Their government embraced non-violent politics, making it difficult to have them on the side of the allied powers. Their military personnel on site, in contrast, would fight at once! Would it be possible one day to find middle around?

"We can try, Brigadier General. Let us give the time to solve this problem on a diplomatic way!" remarked Sir Robertson.

"We can try," nodded General Ganeval, perplexed. "However, I would like to quote your Winston Churchill: *Concerning our Russian friends, there is nothing they admire as much as strength, and there is nothing for which they have less respect than weakness, in particular military weakness.*"

Brigadier General Ganeval was a passionate man.

"Come down, Jean!" General Koenig intervened at once. He shared his military commander's point of view. He adopted, though, a more moderate approach. "Let them negotiate! We will do our best from our side, Generals. We will engage in continuous diplomatic pressure in order to obtain the dismantling of the radio towers. Right, Jean?"

"Bien entendu, mon General!"

General Clay and Sir Robertson relaxed. They would be able to avoid unnecessary complications.

"Mother! Look at that!" Johann pointed toward the elegant cars rushing alongside the runway that was under construction. Trudi turned her head and recognized the most important military commanders in Berlin.

God bless them! Our future depends on these men, she thought.

Chapter 33
Hollywood Glamour

John's squadron arrived to the Fassberg Airbase some weeks ago. After a difficult beginning, the situation improved each day. John walked the path leading from the base in Fassberg to the hunting lodge. Hermann Göring, the powerful commander of the Luftwaffe, the Nazi Air Force, used the hunting lodge when he stayed sometimes at the Training Center, built in the middle of the forest in the mid 1930s. During the war, two hundred Russian prisoners sentenced to labor extended the training school, where almost all types of German aircraft flew.

The U.S. Air Force and the RAF shared the air base. The Americans, in particular, were satisfied with the equipment. Nine hangars for aircraft and a big deposit of fuel were housed in the substantial buildings, along with an officer club, indoor swimming pool and exercise room. In addition, the arrival of the Americans gave a new upswing to the neighborhood.

The British RAF occupied half of the barracks. The rudimentary organization and the limited ration of food were unbelievable for the Americans. They had stewed tomatoes for breakfast and meat pie for dinner. Everyday, they had the same. John admired these British pilots, who did eight to ten hours of duty with nothing in their stomachs. He thought they were the heroes of the airlift. The German workers had more in their bowls than these young British men did. John and the American crews became acquainted with many of the RAF troops, and felt embarrassed to eat fresh beef, chicken and eggs while the British did not have any of those delicacies. John often gave half of his hamburger sandwich to one of them.

John entered the former hunting lodge, called "Flynn's Inn" by the pilots and crewmembers. He went to the bar and ordered a beer. Flynn's Inn was warm. The jukebox played the latest pop songs direct from America. He remembered the officer club and the hunting lodge at his arrival at the base. In spite of the good strong equipment, the American experience in Fassberg was a disaster at the beginning. The surroundings were depressing, in desperate need of renewal. Until the day when Colonel Jack Coulter became commandant of the base and his wife, Connie arrived with him. Connie was Constance Bennett, the famous movie star from Hollywood who was also a wealthy woman.

That night, Connie Bennett was sitting at one of the tables in company of Sir Freddie Laker. The English lord owned twelve converted Halifax bombers. When the British government asked him if they could use his bombers for the airlift, he immediately put the planes at their disposal. The eccentric lord and his civilian crews were well-known celebrities at the base. As usual, Sir Laker's loud laughs filled Flynn's Inn lodge this evening.

Constance Bennett beckoned to John and offered him a seat at the table. John admired Constance Bennett. She transformed the base. New furniture arrived, German workers painted the lodge and the officer club, and she organized parties and recreational escapes. Her healthy laugh and everlasting temperament shined all over the base. John and the other crewmembers called her simply, "Connie". Constance Bennett brought with her the glamour of Hollywood to Fassberg.

Colonel Coulter occupied several command positions in America after his participation in World War II. As training officer in charge, he was involved in the making of training films for pilots and crewmembers. The filming took place in California and he met Constance Bennett in the studio. Constance Bennett accompanied her husband to Europe and subordinated all her activities to the service of the airlift. The Fassberg base was never the same after her arrival.

Today, the evening was as pleasant as usual. The company left Flynn's Inn and in the best mood went back together to the base. The Fassberg base operated twenty-four hours and as always the traffic was at its highest. The situation of the base was ideal. Close to the Ruhr, which was the main source of coal, the most important item for the survival of Berlin, the base was the terminus of several railroads repaired and in part extended by the allied forces. The German Civil Labor Organization ensured the cooperation of five thousand German workers. They lived in the neighborhood of the base in tents and cabins.

Colonel Jack Coulter saw his wife and John, and beckoned them from far. He managed the growing jump traffic himself. Constance Bennett went with quick steps to her husband. Jack Coulter was upset.

"Sergeant, what is it? Why did you stop the takeoffs? Aircraft are accumulating and the taxiways are all full!"

"The visibility is too low, Colonel."

"Do not be foolish! We've had heavier fog before and we did not stop takeoffs!"

"It is not us, Colonel. The young pilot in the Skymaster, there, is arguing a technical problem. He is muttering something about inoperative warning lights. It is his responsibility to take off or refuse to do so."

"Did I hear you right, Sergeant? Let me check that plane!"

Colonel Coulter, Connie and John hurried to the flight line to see what might be wrong with the aircraft. After looking over the Skymaster with care, Colonel Coulter exclaimed.

"This bird is all right! I can fly it to Berlin right now!"

Colonel Coulter climbed into the left seat to take the controls, Connie slipped into the copilot's seat and John became the navigator.

"Let us go!" said Colonel Coulter.

The triumvirate hauled ten tons of coal to the blockaded city.

The whole base, pilots, crewmembers and German workers were all outside, when their plane landed some hours later. They were proud of their Commandant and they were proud to have a Hollywood movie star of character with them. John felt honored to be member of the trio.

Chapter 34
The Radio Towers

Brigadier General Jean Ganeval tapped his finger on the table. Tegel airport began to serve what it was designed for. The first aircraft were arriving at regular intervals. They could not optimize the operation though because of the two Soviet radio towers still represented a major danger in the final approach path. The French specialists and officers were waiting for his decision.

"How long have I said that the Soviets would do nothing?" Brigadier General Ganeval was upset. "The Americans and the British are still thinking they will succeed with negotiation!"

His aid-de-camp nodded.

"We sent several letters and requests. We also started negotiation with our Soviets counterparts. They cannot blame us for that situation!"

"*Par bleu!* Of course, they cannot blame us! I want to use our airport. If we are unable to exploit its operation at full extent, why did we build it?" Jean Ganeval jumped on his feet and pointed to the empty runway through the window.

Captain Claude Leclaire was calm.

"*Mon General,* we are ready. Our team is already waiting for your orders. We can settle this question at once."

Jean Ganeval observed the leader of the French specialists in explosives for a moment. He was right. They were wasting their time. *Direct action, what the Soviets understand,* he thought.

"Okay. Let us start. Tomorrow morning, we will proceed. This operation is secret until completion!"

The officers present hurrahed and shook hands. Jean Ganeval once again felt the excitement of the covert actions of the resistance.

At those times, he went into action against the German Army. Today, he initiated this action in the interest of the Berliners.

The two radio towers, broadcasting hard-line communist propaganda against the Western powers, belonged to Radio Berlin. This situation was unacceptable.

Next morning, after Tegel opened for business, a group of French soldiers marched to the towers. With arms at the ready, they entered the towers and evacuated the personnel. Surprise was complete. The personnel of Radio Berlin followed the instructions, astonished. Before understanding, they stood in the Soviet sector. During this time, specialists positioned explosives at the base of the towers. In less than an hour, the French finished their preparations and created a huge explosion. The two radio towers disappeared; the final approach was clear.

Back at the base, knowing how to celebrate a courageous act, the French waited for their comrades with champagne. They were not alone in their celebration. The Berliners yelled and threw their berets and hats in the air. *Yuppie!* They had waited a long time for decisive action against Radio Berlin. Now, it was silent for twelve hours.

Marshal Kotikov, the Military Commander of the Soviet Sector of Berlin was angry. The French action took them by surprise. He rushed to the office of his French counterpart without notice. He was in the company of two interpreters. One interpreter was in charge to ensure the translations. The second interpreter controlled what the first interpreter translated. The Soviets did not trust anybody.

Jean Ganeval was calm. His face was as marble. He listened to the agitated Soviet delegation. He underlined that the Soviets had ample time to solve the problem. They ignored his requests and therefore the French Commandment had no other option. The French Administration was in charge of security of airplanes landing at Tegel Airport. Moreover, the actions did not threaten lives. The Soviet delegation left without obtaining any reparations.

As soon as the Soviet delegation left, the telephone rang. Frank Howley, Commandant of the American sector was on the line.

"You are crazy, Brigadier General! Did you hear? Now, the Soviets threaten us with interruption of telephone liaison in the Western sectors. Our communications will be endangered."

Brigadier General Jean Ganeval was stone-faced as with the Soviets some minutes ago.

"I do not agree with you. That is a threat and nothing more. They are not able to carry it out. The interruption of telephone cables between Berlin and the Western sectors would destroy the Soviet communication lines as well. In fact, the telephone cables of the Eastern sectors pass through West Berlin. Therefore, they are not in the position to do anything."

The French were right. After the incident, the Soviets did not implement any reprisals. Popularity of the French Armed Forces was at its highest level.

Chapter 35
The Elections

Hans Stolzer opened the folder on his desk and rubbed his fingers. The office was cold. Technical services had shut down the heating system in the offices of the city hall. He tightened his coat and arranged the woolen cap on his head. With the scarf, he made a second wrap around his neck. In the shadows of the winter, candles replaced electricity even in the city hall. He placed the candles nearer to the folder and he began to read the note in it concerning the organization of the upcoming elections.

Berliners have a quick mouth and a self-deprecating cynical view of the world. In the last years, however, they became politically sophisticated. The experts in propaganda wooed them and they had to learn to look behind the banners and slogans. Hans Stolzer was convinced that the Berliners would use the ballot, the sole means at their disposal, to protest against the Soviet Union and the German communists.

The door opened and Willy Brandt, the young associate of Ernst Reuter entered the office.

"Good morning, Hans. I have big news! Konrad Adenauer is flying to West Berlin to support the election campaign."

"That is excellent, Willy!" Hans Stolzer lighted up. "His presence will prove the support of West Germany to West Berlin. We need to underline our liaison with the democratic organizations."

"Yes, this support is important. Did you hear Radio Berlin? They organized a celebration in the Opera House for their recently nominated Magistracy."

"I heard that, yes. They implemented this Opera Magistracy without election. I think it will lighten our work here, I hope. Now, we have two distinct Magistracies. They will not be able to interfere in our organization."

"I am not as optimistic, Hans."

Willy Brandt had concerns. In the last weeks, the Soviet counter-propaganda intensified. During the election campaign, they experienced several disturbances.

"I think the nomination of that Opera Magistracy without doubt splits our town in two. We will need the support of the democratic world more than ever."

"I would not be concerned about that," offered Hans Stolzer. "We had enough proof of their support, right here, above our heads!"

"Yes, you're right."

There was silence for a moment. Hans broke the stillness. "Willy, we have to go, otherwise, we will be late. When will Konrad Adenauer arrive?"

"He will land in a few moments. Let's concentrate on the task. Ernst will pick him up at the new airport in Tegel and they will come together to the ceremony in the French sector."

The two men went to the military jeep reserved for city hall. The first snow covered the streets. Passengers waited in long lines at the streetcar stops. The streetcar company often replaced streetcars with busses. The airlift provided tires and fuel for them.

The car turned into the Bernauer Strasse and continued toward the French sector. Bernauer Strasse separated two districts, Mitte in the East in the Soviet zone, and Wedding in the West, part of the French sector. Soviet soldiers occupied the middle of the street. They were installing barbed wire to mark the limit of the sectors.

"Look at that," told Willy Brandt to Hans Stolzer. "Now, they will establish a border in the middle of the town!"

"Are you surprised, Willy?" Hans turned his eyes toward his young colleague. "In the last months, they instituted passport and visa verification. It is clear that they intend to split the town in two. From a certain point of view, it is even better than the vague organization we had."

"Yeah, it is better to know on what feet we will dance."

In the meantime, they arrived to the meeting in Wedding. When they entered the building, the first person running toward them was Esther Kohlberg.

"Hi, Esther, how are you doing?" greeted her Hans Stolzer. "Let me introduce to you Willy Brandt from the office of Ernst Reuter."

"I am glad to meet you, Willy!" Esther turned toward Hans at once. "I arranged everything according to your request. The fliers are in their chairs and we have two ushers at the entrance helping people to find their places. There are some people here though, whose behavior is strange. Nobody knows them."

"Hmmm... We have to prepare for some disturbances once again. Last week we had provocateurs in Charlottenburg and Spandau in the British sector, and in Neukölln in the American sector. We have to be vigilant."

"Do you want me to call the police?" asked Esther.

"Let us wait and see," answered Hans.

"I do not agree with you," intervened Willy Brandt. "Today, we have a special meeting. Konrad Adenauer and Ernst Reuter will arrive in any moment. I would advocate calling the police. They could be stationed in back of the meeting room. If something would happen, they will be already here."

"You are right, Willy. Do not take any risks! Esther, could you arrange that?"

"Of course, I'll go right away."

The two men entered the meeting room, while Esther ran to the office. This election meeting was important. News of the arrival of Konrad Adenauer and Ernst Reuter spread fast.

Hans recognized Bob Howard in the crowd. The journalist wanted to be at the center of the events. The Americans and the international community followed the election campaign in West Berlin with great interest.

"Hi, Bob! How are you doing?" Hans greeted the well-known newsman. "Willy, Esther, I wish to introduce you Bob Howard, American freelance journalist," said Hans. "Bob, this is Willy Brandt, associate of Ernst Reuter, and let me introduce to you my good friend, Esther Kohlberg. Esther, please find a place for Bob. Bob, stay with us. You are welcome in our group."

"I would not miss that for anything," replied Bob. "I have a lot of questions and perhaps I will have even more after that meeting. We are interested to a great extent in the elections in West Berlin."

"Hans," whispered Esther, "I organized as we discussed. The police are outside at the main entrance in case disturbances would take place."

"Very good, Esther, thank you," said Hans. Esther was a jewel. Hans turned his attention to the organization of the meeting and let his friends take their places in the crowd.

The apprehension of Hans Stolzer found justification as soon as Professor Theodor Heuss stepped to the stand.

"The Berliner elections are an integral part of the democratic process developing in Germany. The moral calories, that Berlin delivers for the West German democracy is more important than the calories sent by West Germany to Berlin!" so, the professor began his discourse.

At that moment, boos shouting and whistles arose in the room. The disturbances came from every corner. Some of the participants wanted to quiet the agitators. Fist fighting followed. The whistle concert continued. People were yelling to each other. Chaos reigned in the whole room. Policemen stormed into the meeting room, isolating the agitators, one by one. They separated around twenty persons and escorted them to an office in the building for interrogation.

At that moment, cars stopped before the building and Ernst Reuter arrived in the company of Konrad Adenauer. The participants welcomed the two men with a hurricane of applause. Their arrival cooled down the participants and their interest turned toward the general issues of the meeting.

The slim and tall Adenauer was one of the most popular political leaders. He became Lord Mayor of Cologne for the first time in 1917. This election made him the youngest mayor in Prussia. He made his name by progressively developing Cologne into a metropolis of the West. His republicanism made from him an object of hate among the adversaries of the republic.

When the Nazis came to power in 1933, they replaced him at once as Lord Mayor of Cologne and banished him from the city of his birth. By the end of the war, the Gestapo imprisoned him for several months as an enemy of the regime following the failed assassination attempt on Hitler.

The victorious Americans reinstated Adenauer into the office of Lord Mayor of Cologne. In 1948, the three Western Allied Powers created the Parliamentary Council and Adenauer became the elected President. The Council was charged to formulate a Constitution for the Federal Republic of Germany.

Adenauer's presence galvanized the crowd participating in the meeting. He arrived at the best moment to counter-balance the communist terror trying to subvert and disturb the free election in the Westerns sectors. He was calm and listened to the orators of the meeting.

"Our conviction is," continued Theodor Heuss, "that the Berliners will vote for western democracy and by that fact, against eastern slavery!"

Konrad Adenauer stepped to the stand.

"We are not permitted to abandon our well earned right for freedom! Those who would be tempted to this idea do not merit to be called German!"

Warm applauses followed his words. He continued with conviction.

"The West German economy is getting out from the worst of it. The time of crisis is behind us, and in the coming months we will see important improvements in our everyday lives. The sole rescue for all of Europe lies in the creation of a European Federation. Germany expresses the wish to be part of that future federation with the same rights and duties as all the other participating countries. These elections are paving the road for international acknowledgement of a new democratic Germany!"

Ernst Reuter closed the line of the intervening orators.

"Despite of the terror actions and the menace exercised by the communists, we count on the large participations of the Berliners on these elections! The Soviet measures did not intimidate the Berliners so far, and we are certain about the protection of the western occupational powers."

The meeting closed on that optimistic tone. When the participants left, the police officer stepped up to Hans Stolzer.

"I think you should know that we verified the identity of the agitators. They are all members of the communist party from East Germany. They are not even Berliners. They received orders for their disruptions, and a bus transported them to Berlin from the provinces of Sachsen and Brandenburg. Since they are not inhabitants of West Berlin, we are not in position to arrest them. All we are able to do is to expel them from West Berlin."

"I am not surprised," answered Hans. "The Soviets have no shame in expanding their terror to intimidate the Berliners from voting. Anyway, I thank you for the information."

Bob Howard stayed with Esther, who had helped him to follow the events of the meeting. He enjoyed the company of that beautiful girl with her musical accent.

"Can I drop you off somewhere?" asked Bob politely.

"I am going to the airport, in Tempelhof," answered Esther. "It is perhaps too far from your destination or your route."

"It is off my route, but I can manage it."

They left together. In the car, they continued to discuss the incidents of the evening.

"These troublemakers are well known figures of our landscape." Esther was happy to give her opinion to Bob Howard. "The communists want to disrupt the election. In the Eastern sectors, many businesses organize a shift called 'Sunday for reconstruction' on the day of the election preventing their employees, inhabitants of the Western sectors, from voting. At the same time, the communist propaganda threatens reprisals for those who are not on the job or might be late to their work on that day."

"What will you do about it?" asked Bob.

"The various non-communist syndicates and the employees of the Berliner Transportation companies declared a strike on that day. Thus, all traffic of West Berlin will close down. The Soviets and the communists would not be able to implement any reprisals to the inhabitants of West Berlin. Berliners will be able to vote at any time. You will see these elections will be a victory. I am confident."

"I think you are always confident," smiled Bob.

In the meantime, they arrived at Tempelhof airport. The airport was busy. The airplanes arrived every three minutes as usual. Bob's professional curiosity was aroused.

"What are you doing so late at the airport?"

"I work here, not tonight though."

She jumped out from the car, without any explanation, and ran to the pilot waiting at the entrance. They fell in each other's arms holding one another tight for a moment. Bob got out of the car and watched them. He leaned back and sat on the bumper, smiling.

Love is growing on strange places, but it is the force of life, he thought. *What an article I will write about this!*

Chapter 36
The Plane Crash

Bob Howard stood in front of the Allied Control Council Building in the Heinrich von Kleist Park. John Carpenter arranged Bob's visit to the BASC, the Berlin Air Safety Center. The young men mutually liked one other and formed a fast friendship. Bob admired John's past as fighter pilot and was enthusiastic about his role in the founding of the Berlin Air Safety Center. Bob's outgoing personality and his investigative spirit impressed John, who kept in touch with his friends from the BASC. Therefore, he was able to organize this visit for his journalist friend at the center. The flags of the four nations were still flying at the main entrance.

Bob Howard crossed the street and entered the imposing building. He had a strange feeling. The four-story building with five hundred and fifty rooms was empty. While a guard accompanied him through the labyrinth of large deserted corridors, he heard the echo of his steps.

"Nobody is here!" exclaimed Bob. "Where are the people? That is a ghost building! At least, that is my impression."

"The Soviets left the Allied Council in March 1948 and all cooperation ceased between the allied powers," answered the soldier. "The Berlin Air Safety Center is the sole common organization still in use and still working in that building. They occupy less than forty rooms here. The building is otherwise empty."

They arrived to the corner of the BASC office complex and guards quarters and at last, they experienced some activity. Here, doors slammed, people ran, and voices mixed up in a whispering chaos. Bob felt relieved. This was something he planned to see and hear.

He was looking for John's friend, Sergeant McNulty, who did a remarkable job as final-approach controller. If Bob wanted to write about GCA, ground-controlled approach, the sergeant is the person who was able to give him the most thorough presentation. The sergeant sat beside one of the numerous screens in the room, concentrating on the moving green points on it. He guided one of the pilots to his final destination. When he saw the guard and Bob, he acknowledged them with a wave and came over to them after completing his job. He never left behind an uncompleted job. He was expecting his visitor.

"Hi! You are Bob Howard, the journalist, I believe." The Sergeant shook Bob's hand. He was an easygoing person. "How is my friend, John doing? He has a beautiful girlfriend. Do you know her?"

"Yes, I know her." he answered.

"She is the most beautiful girl on the Tempelhof airport," added Sergeant McNulty. "What a lucky guy is this John!"

"I am sure of that," underlined Bob.

"I understood from John that you are interested in the technical support of the airlift."

"Yes, indeed. It is perhaps the most important element of the airlift, I believe," nodded Bob.

"I'll be happy to guide you through our Center," responded the Sergeant. "You have to know that the Berlin Air Safety Center is the initial connection for air traffic control. We pass the information to the Approach Control Centers at the Berlin airfields. The Approach Control Centers consist of both fixed and mobile units around the airfields."

Sergeant McNulty was beaming, exuding enthusiasm about the airlift and the exploits of the ground-controlled approach. They traversed the adjacent rooms. They were in the nerve central of the airlift. The controllers overlooked the crowded air corridors. They did not have sophisticated landing aids at their disposal. They had compass, altimeter, altitude, and speed indicators. They were staring hour after hour into the flickering green tubes. At any time and in any weather conditions, instrument flying was the rule.

The situation was difficult for everybody. The young recruits were inexperienced. The more experienced controllers did not face these crowded air corridors conditions either. It was the first time in the history of aviation that controllers had to manage that number and that frequency of flights. After the opening of the new Tegel airport, they had a plane landing every minute in Berlin.

"Sergeant," said Bob with a big open smile on his face, "you are making us believe that this job is one of aviation's milestones!"

"That is fact, Bob," retorted the Sergeant. "It is the milestone! Aviation will never be the same after the airlift. One day, flying will be popular and perhaps millions and millions will travel through crowded airports. The airlift and our GCA units are paving the road of the future."

"What enthusiasm you have, Sergeant!" Bob Howard was smiling with pleasure on the futuristic vision of the Sergeant. He admired this lowly soldier for his dream with wide-opened eyes.

All of a sudden, trembling voice and scary words cut through the whispering chaos.

"Mayday... Mayday! We have engine failure... I repeat — Mayday, Mayday, we have engine failure."

Sergeant McNulty ran to the screen at once. Bob followed him. Fear mounted in the center.

"Which plane is that?" asked the Sergeant.

"It's a four-engine Skymaster, Sergeant; Lieutenant John Carpenter and his crew," answered the controller.

Sergeant McNulty and Bob looked at each other. Bob's face became white. He had not counted on the possibility that something could happen to his friend. He even less had counted on the possibility that it would happen before his eyes.

"Where are they?"

"Deep in the Soviet zone, halfway between Wiesbaden and Tempelhof."

Sergeant McNulty guessed Bob's thoughts.

"They are in difficulty, but John is an experienced pilot," he said.

"This is flight 174. Mayday... Mayday. We are unable to maintain altitude. We are crashing — I repeat, it is flight 174. We are crashing — Engine failure..."

"Flight 174. Save yourself. Jump!"

"Mayday... Mayday..."

"Flight 174. Flight 174." The controller repeated the identification, but he no longer received any answer. Communications were lost.

Personnel in the Operations Room stopped their work for a moment. While the controllers took back their job, Sergeant McNulty was thinking. *What would be the best way to learn the crew's whereabouts?* He hoped they had the chance to parachute. In that case, they would be in the Soviet zone. *What would happen to them?* He rushed to the Soviet members of the Berlin Air Safety Center, a controller and an interpreter. Bob followed him.

"Sergeant, do you think you will be able to negotiate with them," Bob asked, anxiously.

"I think so, yes," answered the Sergeant. "Besides safety of air traffic, one of the missions of the Center is to ensure the security of the crews."

Captain Sortschenko was the Chief Soviet officer in the BASC. The two men entered his office at once. He was accustomed to negotiations with the American and British officers. He treated all the claims related to the Soviet harassments in the air corridors on an everyday basis. The allied officers reported each break of the rules defined in the signed covenant. As usual, Captain Sortschenko demonstrated no reaction. The Americans had to wait and see for the verdict of the Soviet Administration. Would they or would they not treat the crew with dignity?

John was the last to jump from the plane. The crew of Flight 174 parachuted in the neighborhood of the small village of Langensalza, in Thüringien. The village was known as a healing spa for its hot saltwater. At this time of the year, the tourists had deserted the village. The inhabitants heard the unfamiliar noise in the sky and noted the plane in distress. Before they could help the pilots, a Soviet military jeep stopped them. The soldiers drove to the crash site at high speed. Some of the inhabitants turned away and took the small path behind the beautiful, gothic-style city hall. Under cover of the bushes, they ran to the forest.

The Soviet soldiers did not waste any time. They encircled the burning plane and hunted for the crew. John Carpenter was entangled in his parachute. The soldiers surrounded him, menacing their weapons. He had no choice but follow them. It took the Soviets two minutes to discover Garry, who had hidden in the bushes. The Soviets tossed the two airmen into their jeep. While the Soviets were in deep discussion, John and Garry tried to give the impression there are no other crewmembers. The Soviets continued to look around, but they were not able to locate Josh and Chuck, and began to believe the crew consisted only of John and Garry. They came back to the jeep and drove back to their quarters in town, holding John and Garry under threat of their weapons.

Josh landed farther on the North in the middle of the forest. He began to look for the other crewmembers at once. He heard the jeep and saw the Soviet soldiers. He held his breath. He did not trust the Soviets; one never knew what they might do next. He could not see the jeep clearly, but had the impression that only two Americans were in it. He moved cautiously and tried to locate the fourth crew member. At that moment, he heard the whisper.

"*Psst.* Come here... Quiet... Russkies there." The local people saw the parachutes. They tried to locate the crew members before the Soviets did. They were ready to help the American crew.

Josh approached the men in the bushes. They held their breath and tried to remain unseen. They saw John and Garry under guard by the soldiers. Josh made signs to the friendly people and they started to look for Chuck as soon as the Soviet jeep drove back to the town. Chuck lay under the trees, with an injured leg and could barely move. The Germans helped him and they moved back taking the pathway through the forest.

In Berlin, at the BASC, Captain Sortschenko went through the usual process. He was not in hurry. The Soviet radar officers already signaled him that the plane was in distress. To avoid confrontation with the Allied Powers, he requested the Intelligence Officer to hand over the American pilots at once. He contemplated the message he received. He went to the door and looked for Sergeant McNulty.

"Sergeant! I have to inform you, we found two crew members. We have no trace of the others." Captain Sortschenko was calm and official. "I am sorry."

Unable to do anything about it, Sergeant McNulty and Bob accepted the answer. They hoped the crews were still alive. Their thoughts went to the young men risking their lives over their heads.

"Do you have their names, Captain?" asked Sergeant McNulty.

"No, I do not have any names," answered the Soviet Captain. "I am sorry."

Sergeant McNulty and Bob exchanged a worried look. They had to continue hoping. Nothing was lost yet.

John and Garry in the jeep noticed that the Soviet Lieutenant received a radio call. By all evidence, the Soviets dropped the search, and tossed the Americans in a cellar. John and Garry worried over the Soviet intentions. They also worried about Josh and Chuck. *What happened to them? Did they make it? Who will help them if they have injuries?*

At the other end of the village, the townspeople accompanied the young airmen to the parish church.

"Reverend, we have to do something for the Americans."

"Of course, let them in."

The Americans did not understand the whispering, but they felt the sympathy of the men and their helpfulness.

"We have to drive them to the western zones. What do you think, Reverend?"

"Yes, but let them dressed as priests and I will drive them. The Soviets are used to seeing me drive all over the countryside."

The Reverend turned toward Josh. "Where are you from?" he asked in a poor English. "What airport are you coming from?"

"Wiesbaden," answered Josh.

"I will drive you back to West Germany."

Josh and Chuck understood by their rescuers' gestures that they had to change into priest garb. In a half an hour, they were ready. The car drove slowly before the city hall toward West. The Soviets did not challenge it. They were busy in their quarters with their prisoners.

John and Garry waited confidently in the cellar. The Soviets could not harm them. *We are not in war after all! This is an accident,* thought John. When the Soviets appeared at the doorstep, the two American airmen found reason to worry though. The Soviets pushed them in a military jeep once again, and drove toward the West. John and Garry began to feel reassured. Two hours later, the Soviets freed the two Americans at the border of West Germany. The authorities already waited them there and after two more hours, they arrived at the Wiesbaden airbase. Their main concern was for Josh and Chuck. Did they make it also? What happened to them? At the base, nobody seemed to know anything about the two other crewmembers.

In the Berlin Air Safety Center, the tension lowered. They already knew about John and Garry. Captain Sortschenko was quick to settle this matter with his superiors. When the next day, the border guards arrested two illegal passengers, everybody felt relieved learning they were Josh and Chuck. This adventure finished for the good.

Bob Howard was once again in the best place to relate an interesting story. *That is perhaps a Cold War, but we have some hot situations,* he thought. Tightening his pilot jacket, he felt honored to be here at these trying times.

Chapter 37
The University

Bob Howard stood in front of the Titania Palast and contemplated the imposing building. At the corner, an illuminated tower about one hundred feet high adorned the building. In the last months, the illuminated tower remained dark though. The electricity shortage did not allow turning on the bulbs arranged in twenty-seven lines.

The Titania Palast was the glamorous movie theater of Berlin, where the first German presentation of film sensations from Hollywood took place in the 1920s and 1930s. The theater was one of the buildings that survived the bombing of the war. The building welcomed the performing arts and concerts. Today, it will host a worldwide event, the foundation of the Free University of Berlin.

The world famous Humboldt University of Berlin was located in the Soviet sector. The Soviets began ousting professors and students who did not conform to the communist ideology. Professors and students arrived at the Western sectors, where, with American assistance, they created the nucleus of the new university, a symbol of academic freedom.

John and Esther arrived holding each other's hand. Happiness shone in their faces. The airlift experienced one of the longest-lasting fogs ever, which blanketed the entire European continent for weeks. Temperature dropped below freezing. That was bad news for Berliners and the allied administration. At one point, the whole city had only one week's supply of coal. That was, though, a godsend for Esther and John. The fog grounded John in Berlin. They never felt as free and as happy in their whole life. They lived for today and the future had plenty of promises made especially for them.

"Hi, Bob! I should play the lottery, as sure as I was certain to meet with you here," said John, and tapped on Bob's shoulder.

"Lucky you!" answered Bob. "You court the prettiest girl in Berlin! How are you, Esther? I am happy to see you again."

"Hi, Bob! Today, Berlin has a date with the world! It is so good to be here," she said, not being able to hold back her enthusiasm. The two young men smiled at her.

They entered the elegant building. The theater opened in 1928 and offered two thousand seventy-one seats. John and Esther had their seat on the balcony on the second floor, not far from the zone reserved for journalists. They motioned to Bob, and they all stared with curiosity at all the important personalities present on that special occasion.

Glossy mahogany paneling decorated the ground floor theater. Three parabolic profiles encircled the stage. Between them, organ pipes added to the ornaments. The royal blue velvet curtain was raised, and silence followed. Behind a beautifully adorned table, the speakers of the evening took their seats.

Ernst Reuter stepped to the microphone and opened the evening.

"The entire world is here tonight to celebrate with all of us, Berliners of free thinking, the foundation and the opening of the Berliner Free University. A system that wants to hold the population of Berlin in ropes and chains, maintaining them in slavery, is robbing and destroying our elementary civil rights."

Ernst Reuter continued with conviction.

"The Berliner Free University is the answer of freedom loving human beings who want to create from it a place of free men in a free city. Our hope is that the Berliner Free University will be the bridge between Berlin and the rest of a free and democratic Germany!"

After the stand-up applause died down, Colonel Frank L. Howley, military commandant of Berlin, followed the Lord Mayor of Berlin. "At first, let me pass on to you congratulations from General Lucius D. Clay, Military Commandant of Germany."

The name of General Lucius D. Clay generated a standing ovation from the audience. Frank Howley continued.

"We all, present here in this room this night, and also those who share our excitement all over the world, hope that this Free University will overcome the ghost of the propaganda rolling toward us from the East!"

The American author, Thornton Wilder, stepped to the microphone. The world famous author felt intimidated by the great distinction bestowed upon him.

"In three weeks, when millions all around the world will prepare for the celebration of Christmas, they will prepare a gift from Germany to the world: the Christmas tree. Under the tree, they will sing a German song, 'Holy Night.' Let us a moment remember that Christmas in 1917, when on the front in their trenches, the soldiers of France, Germany, Britain and America sang the same song, in the same time, each in their mother language. Today, we do not need to sing this universal song to feel our connection."

The famous author knew how to speak tears into the eyes of the audience. He continued his discourse with eloquence.

"The little man of the street from America is here. A part of him is flying to Berlin with each sack of flour, with each bag of coal and with each dollar spent for the reconstruction of Germany. In the name of this little man of the street and on behalf of the American universities, congratulations to the Berliner Free University and welcome in our world!"

The applause went not only to Thornton Wilder but also to the little man of the street in America evoked by the famous author.

The festivity concluded with the discourse of Professor Redslob from the Berliner Fee University.

"We have no more than a few minutes remaining of the electricity supply. After our celebration, darkness will reign once again in this theater and on Berlin. However, through that darkness, the light of knowledge will shine for long times to come. Let me close this celebration with the words of Goethe, one of the greatest German writers: From today and from this place there begins a new epoch in the history of the world."

John, Esther and Bob left the theater in an emotional atmosphere, not saying a word. It was not necessary. The eloquence of the orators said everything.

Chapter 38
Merry Christmas

Gerd Eberhardt stood in the garden in front of the small pine tree with an ax in hand. Trudi was beside him and she placed her hands on his shoulder.

"It will be fine, Gerd," she reassured him. "We will plant another one next year."

They wanted to prepare a Christmas tree, but to purchase one was much too expensive. They wanted to take just a branch from that pine tree, but the cold was severe in the last weeks and they were not able to heat the mansion. The extra twenty-five pounds of coal distributed by the administration would not hold out long. They burned all the dried branches they were able to find in the garden. Cutting down this tree, would ensure a merry Christmas and after the holiday, they will be able to heat the kitchen for several days.

For the moment, they wanted to prepare their Christmas tree as a surprise for the children. Shadows of the afternoon came fast at this season of the year. They had to be quick. They limited the decoration to some golden bulbs and candles. They waited for the electricity to begin their celebration though. They adored the Christmas for the romantic atmosphere provided by the candles. This year, however, they had candlelight every afternoon and night. The candlelight lost all his romantic influence. Today, they would celebrate Christmas with the bright light of the increased ration of electricity provided by the military administration.

The children were at the school, where they had Christmas celebration in presence of Santa Claus. This year, Santa Claus was present in all schools and hospitals in West Berlin. Those Santa Clauses, however, did not speak German. The soldiers and officers of the American garrisons in Berlin took the costume of Santa Claus and participated in the celebration. Their baskets were full with chocolates, bonbons, and candy bars sent by the American nation to the children of West Berlin.

The delighted children of the Eberhardt family accompanied by Esther arrived from the school. Little Fritz entered holding hand with a Santa Claus. John arranged to be the Santa Claus in their school. Little Fritz was happy and proud to present his Santa Claus friend to all his schoolmates. Anna, and even the oldest Johann, felt special knowing this young American pilot playing the role of Santa Claus with conviction and enthusiasm.

They arrived at the mansion when Bob Howard stopped his car, and with quick steps entered the house. John obtained tickets for them in the American garrison of Berlin. They would attend the Christmas party organized by the military administration. While John got out from the Santa Claus costume, Bob had a conversation with Esther.

"Esther, you were right concerning the elections. Eighty-six percent participation is the highest percentage I have ever seen!"

"You see, I told you! I was sure the Berliners would vote for freedom in spite of the terror exerted by the Soviets."

The Eberhardt family knew Bob Howard; they were happy to see the sociable American journalist.

"What do you wish for Christmas?" asked Bob.

"I think a warm bath would be luxurious," answered Trudi. "I would like also to prepare fresh potatoes instead of these dehydrated flakes. Everything is in powder from potatoes to milk. Did you hear the joke on RIAS? 'Decorations for Christmas would be no problem, the Allies would fly in powdered Christmas trees that could be reconstituted with water.' We had a true Christmas tree though, you see."

The rich laugh filled in the kitchen, the only heated room in the mansion. The Americans and Esther were leaving, when Mister Kupfer, the eighty-year-old neighbor knocked on the door. He put his glasses on to see better in the shadowy late afternoon in the candlelight.

"I am happy to see you, John. I came to see you…"

"Herr Kupfer, good afternoon and Merry Christmas!"

"Thank you! I would like to give you a Christmas gift, my son," said Mister Kupfer. He took out a small box from his pocket and gave it to John. John opened the box carefully. In the box, lay a pocket watch. Everyone in the room has seen it in the hand of Mister Kupfer several times.

"I cannot accept this, Herr Kupfer," exclaimed John. "You could get a small fortune for it on the black market! You would be able to live on it for a month, perhaps even longer. Why would you give me this watch?"

"That is a small token from an old and grateful heart. I would like you to take it. Thank you for the buzz in the sky. Please, accept it, Son."

Bob and Esther had tears on the eyes. John hesitated a moment and after, he embraced the old man. He put the watch in his pocket.

"I will always keep it with me, Herr Kupfer. Thank you and happy Christmas to you."

The moment was touching, the young people had to leave right away though. The Christmas party in the garrison would not wait. They wanted to arrive there before complete darkness. Esther was overjoyed in the car.

"That is so interesting! You know, that is a real performance as in a theater! I have never seen a live performance! I have been in movie theater in Wiesbaden, but I had never experienced this before!"

The Americans smiled at her and were proud to present to her the American art of entertainment. Bob Howard turned into the McNair Allee and headed toward the American garrison in the Goerzallee. General Lucius D. Clay also would be present on the entertainment provided by Irving Berlin and Bob Hope from the United States.

When they entered the entertainment room in the garrison, Bob stopped them. "Wait a minute! You look so great tonight! This is a good moment to make a picture of you together. Stand here..." Bob directed them toward a column and arranged for the photo.

"Cheese!"

John and Esther smiled.

"Bob! When can I have the photo?" inquired Esther.

"I will give a print to each of you as soon as I prepare them. Next week, I think."

They took their place and applauded when the performance began. Irving Berlin and Bob Hope appeared on the scene.

"Ladies and Gentlemen, Mister Irving Berlin," introduced Bob Hope.

"No, you got the name wrong! It is Irving Jones!"

"Irving Jones? What is that?"

"Yes, I changed it! Anything over here named Berlin they cut up into sectors!"

Esther was happy to be here. She enjoyed every moment of the evening. Amongst the healthy laughs, she remembered her childhood and the wonderful moments spent with the family. The human spirit is marvelous. In all hopeless situations, people find the way to hope, to laugh, and to believe. She believed that despite all difficulties, these men here in that room would become victorious, and without bloodshed. This Army consisting of Santa Claus, this Army that transports vital supplies, this Army that is saving the lives of two and half million inhabitants — that Army brings life instead of destruction.

Chapter 39
In Paris

The train arrived in the morning on the *Gare de l'Est,* the Eastern Rail Station in Paris. Bob Howard took the night train from Frankfurt. He was in Paris after the victory four years ago, and he was particularly happy to come back now. Paris had an unrivalled atmosphere. He left the station and stopped at the main gate overlooking the Boulevard Magenta. At this early hour, the streets were still empty. The bars around the station were opened. The waiters cleaned the tables.

He entered the bar at the corner and ordered a French breakfast, black coffee, and croissants. He enjoyed this black coffee, strong and tasty. The croissants were still warm. *What a delight,* he thought. The words of Hemingway about Paris being a moveable feast came into his mind. The time spent in Paris marked the young Hemingway. Bob took a deep breath and enjoyed the smell of Paris. *Yes, Hemingway was right.*

Bob Howard reserved a hotel in the district of the Opera, not far from Harry's Bar, the well-known American bar in Paris. One of the most famous bars in the world, birthplace of the brilliant *Bloody Mary,* Harry's had been serving superlative cocktails since 1911. The clientele of the bar was the cosmopolitan, sophisticated, and chic elite of the French capital.

Bob did not waste his time. After he checked in, he headed at once toward the *Palais Chaillot,* headquarter of the United Nations. He obtained his press certificate and studied the program of the sessions. He walked outside, to the esplanade of the Trocadero facing the Eiffel Tower on the other side of the Seine. He took a deep breath to feel even in his stomach this unequaled atmosphere of Paris.

171

The Palais Chaillot sheltered the World Exposition of 1937. A central terrace with gilded bronze statues linked two enormous pavilions, which stretched in two wings, as a long, curving embrace. From here, a wonderful complex of terraces, staircases, and gardens descended toward the Seine: an oasis of green, enlivened by the sound of waterfalls and the splashes of water jets.

Bob contemplated for a moment the beautiful landscape. His senses drank in every element of it. He drew up his plan of investigation. He turned back into the main building and went right to the press representation office. It was beside the restaurant and coffee shop in the prestigious palace. Where else could one find journalists? According to his experience, that was the best place to set off a path in the search for the truth.

The United Nation was in turmoil for several months now. The Berlin crisis occupied the majority of the sessions. Diplomats wanted to find a peaceful solution to the problem. At the beginning of the hostilities, the United Nations had hoped to organize a meeting between President Truman and Generalissimo Stalin. The efforts of the diplomats failed and finished in a dead end. The two leaders exchanged telegrams though. Truman tirelessly repeated his request for the cancellation of the blockade and Stalin stubbornly repeated the technical difficulties faced by the Soviet Administration.

Several months went on from that time, but the position of the two political blocks did not change an iota. Bob entered the balcony reserved for the press and observed the diplomats present in the big conference room. Argentina was the President of the actual session. Juan Attilio Bramuglia, the Argentine diplomat stood at the stand. He gave the floor to the first speaker, Sir Alexander Cadogan of the British Delegation.

Sir Alexander Cadogan explained the negotiations in process in order to find compromises between the allied powers and the Soviet Union. The intervention of the Security Council would be necessary.

After the British intervention, the U.S. representative, Senator Warren Austin, expressed concerns of the United States. The Soviet Union did not even try to initiate a meeting of the Ministers of Foreign

Affairs before the implementation of the Berlin Blockade. The Berlin blockade is a unilateral decision and therefore unacceptable.

The French representative, Alexandre Parodi, underlined that the Soviet Administration had enough time to solve their technical difficulties if such was to be their intention.

Somebody tapped on Bob's shoulder. It was Kingsbury Smith from the International News Service.

"Look at the Soviet Representative. There..." and he pointed to Andrej Wyschinskij. Wyschinskij pushed his left arm forward and supported his chin on it. Now and then, he made notes on the paper before him. He chewed a long pencil. He was as mysterious and immobile as a Sphinx, yet ready to jump to defend his government at any moment. Behind his eyeglasses, he stared into emptiness. Nobody was able to see any reaction on his behavior.

Kingsbury Smith looked over the conference room. His eyes ran over the seats and representatives. He did not see the leaders of the two most important delegations — Philip Jessup from the USA, and Jacob Malik from the Soviet Union. Neither was present at that session. *Was that a sign? Was it possible that secret negotiations were in process?*

"Come on, Bob! Let us have a drink!"

The two journalists left the balcony and chatted about the latest news in their respective lives.

Next day, Bob met his French friends, Claude and Ginette. They spent the evening together in the Saint Germain des Près. Bob adored the *Quartier Latin* with its intellectual atmosphere, the crowd of students and artists. They were sitting on the terrace of *Café Flore* sipping red wine. The discussion quickly turned to the German question. Bob's experience in Germany and especially in West Berlin, interested Claude and Ginette.

"Look, Bob, in Germany, as everywhere," said Ginette, "there are good people and bad people. I am sure that my fellow Frenchmen think this way. They have the right to rebuild their country."

"Ginette, you are right," nodded Claude. "I would like, though, to underline that it will be necessary to control German industry of the Ruhr region. This region supplied military equipment for Germany twice in the last fifty years. The Germans can rebuild their country, but this reconstruction has to be in a decentralized Germany without new threats to the peace in Europe!"

"I have come from Germany." Bob listened, astonished, at the remarks. He awaited a broader standpoint from his friends. "The German people in the Western zones of Germany, and in particular in West Berlin, want to live in democracy. Nazism is beyond doubt, dead. I met with Konrad Adenauer and he firmly wants to establish French-German negotiations. The Germans want cooperation in Europe and want to be part of a new European Federation."

"Bob," responded Claude, "I do believe that there are political circles in Germany striving for French-German cooperation and through it, for the creation of a real European Federation. We suffered too much from German militarism. Let us have proof of their intentions!"

Bob was disappointed. He was enthusiastic about West Berlin, about the new political development in Germany. He had to realize that knowledge of these changes were not widespread in Europe. This new European Federation had years to take form.

Bob passed over his concerns and concentrated on the forthcoming meeting of the Defense Ministers in Paris. Among other celebrities was Senator Arthur Vandenberg, who arrived to Paris from Michigan. The senator's resolution introduced the year before shaped new defense politics in the United States, accepting America's international role in opposing the spread of Communism.

The United States was ready to participate in a regional security pact under the United Nations Charter. The already made collective arrangements would lead to the finalization of the North Atlantic Treaty Organization, NATO, during this meeting.

Bob was proud to be in Paris during these days. During the press conference, he discussed once again in detail his impressions with his friend from the International News Service organization. Kingsbury Smith was distraught though. Once again, he did not see Philip

Jessup or Jacob Malik. The American and the Soviet diplomats were distant in these last days. Kingsbury Smith already had some information on the secret negotiations in process. An eventual agreement ending the Berlin crisis and resulting in lifting of the blockade would be an international event that would lead to a peace. That was the wish of everybody here in Paris.

When Bob jumped in the train some days later, he did not know that the airlift implemented by the U.S. Air Force and the British RAF was at the point of breaking the blockade and forcing the retreat of the Soviet Union. For him, the outcome of the Berlin crisis was still uncertain.

Chapter 40

In Stalin's Study

Yuri Modin, the enigmatic officer of the Soviet Intelligence Service, traversed Ivanovsky Square in the Kremlin leading to the building of the Presidium. He stopped a moment at the Tsar cannon, the largest cannon of the world. This cast-iron vestige of Russian history stood in front of the building, emanating everlasting steadiness. He hurried up the imposing staircase of the Presidium. The building housed a military school for officers of the Red, then the Soviet Army before becoming the official building of the Soviet Supreme. Joseph Stalin had his quarters here. Yuri Modin's heart beat faster. He pressed the folder in his hand and was extremely proud of its content. This folder would open the door to the General Secretary.

Only privileged persons knew the name included in the anonymous folder. Donald Maclean was the secret weapon of the Soviet Union. The British diplomat was the son of a Scottish politician, Sir Donald Maclean, a distinguished member of the Parliament. The pampered son went on to Cambridge University, where he met Kim Philby, Guy Burgess, and Anthony Blunt, all of them fervent partisans of communism. The KGB had no difficulty in recruiting them. Donald Maclean became one of the most important spies of the Soviet Union. Through his father's connection, he obtained a position at the Foreign Office, and provided numerous reports of high value to the Soviets.

Yuri Modin met Donald Maclean in New York during the years of war. Yuri Modin detested Donald Maclean. The drunk, instable and cowardly traitor escaped by a hair's breadth the net prepared by the Chief Officer of the CIA, James Angleton, at the last moment. Maclean gave up his job in the nuclear committee, but stayed in Washington and continued to provide information that passed through the British Embassy. All information transmitted by Donald Maclean was classified, and very sensitive intelligence.

Yuri Modin arrived to the offices of Joseph Stalin and waited his call. The mahogany covered walls were warm and the interior was elegant. He felt in some extent intimidated though. It was important for him to make a good impression. The door opened and he entered the office of the Man of Steel.

"*Zdravsvuytye*, Comrade General Secretary," whispered Yuri Modin. He noticed being alone with Stalin. The General Secretary wanted to receive his information in secret. That was a good sign for the intelligence officer.

Stalin nodded and showed the seat at his desk.

"Comrade General Secretary," began Yuri Modin, "I have received new information related to the Berlin Blockade."

Stalin nodded once again, but did not say a word. He was waiting.

"The United States considered the possibility of using the A-Bomb if a transport plane was shot down by Soviet artillery fire or if Soviet troops marched on West Berlin."

"Is this information through the person we both know?" asked Stalin.

"Yes, Comrade General Secretary."

"What is the KGB analysis concerning this matter?" inquired Stalin.

"They did not use any military means at their disposal until now. It is true that, besides the harassments in the air corridors, we did not carry out any military action either."

"What do you think, personally?"

Yuri Modin became nervous. It was extremely difficult to give advice to Stalin. If Stalin did not like it, the advisor could finish-up in a gulag within the hour. Yuri Modin was sweating.

"They have the material possibility. They have the Bomb, and in England they have B-29 bombers capable of carrying it. I do not believe though, Comrade General Secretary. As long as we avoid direct confrontation, they will not use the Bomb."

Stalin leaned back in his seat, thinking. The Berlin blockade contributed to the creation of the new regional defense alliance with the purpose of defending Western Europe against possible attack by Communist nations. It was as uncomfortable as the news concerning the A-bomb. Stalin was even more worried.

"They have, though, this new organization," remarked Stalin.

"Yes, Comrade General Secretary. They signed the North Atlantic Treaty Organization on April 4, 1949. It is now officially in place, Comrade General Secretary." Yuri Modin was despaired. What would happen to him? His hopes for advancement seemed to be evaporating.

Stalin got up and walked all around in the office with his cigarette in hand. He was disgusted. He intended the Berlin blockade to be the means of shutting down the Western powers and taking all Germany into the Soviet zone of influence. He went to the window and contemplated Red Square. He had wanted a major victory, and now he had barely the possibility to save face in front of the Americans.

The counter-blockade implemented by the Western powers stopped all deliveries to the Soviet zone, and through that, to the Soviet Union. In the last months, the allies even strengthened the counter-blockade. The black market was not able to deliver anything. Whole industries came to a standstill.

"How this airlift is going?" asked Stalin nervously, walking back to his desk. Yuri Modin felt the nervousness mounting in the room. The fear squeezed his heart.

"They realize a new record everyday. The allied administrations raised the food ration in West Berlin because of the increased tonnage delivered to the town. General Tunner declared an Easter parade for Sunday, April 16, 1949, with objective to haul thirteen thousand tons to Berlin," reported the intelligence officer.

"And did they make it?" asked Stalin when he was tapping his finger on his desk.

"They hauled only twelve thousand, nine hundred and forty tons in one thousand, three hundred and ninety-eight flights without a single accident or incident," answered Yuri Modin.

"What? Then, they made it! What is the difference of sixty tons?"

Stalin realized that the Allies were determined to stay in Berlin and that further blockade was useless. The Allies were ready to maintain the airlift for years if necessary. He had to begin serious negotiations and to comply with a settlement on Allied terms. How would he be able to save face in that situation? That was the single outstanding question. He called the responsible diplomat from the Soviet Foreign Ministry. Vladimir Yerofeyev arrived at once.

Yerofeyev noticed the upset atmosphere and his face became white. He saw the intelligence officer and was alarmed about the next question.

"What is the state of our negotiations with the allies?" inquired Stalin.

"They accept negotiations if we lift the blockade," answered Yerofeyev. "That would mean, we accept the introduction of the new currency, the D-Mark in West Germany, and in West Berlin and we accept the creation of a federal German state."

"Could we begin the negotiations and remove the blockade after?" asked Stalin.

"Comrade General Secretary, that is not possible. The allied position is clear in that respect — No negotiation before the end of the blockade," affirmed Yerofeyev. He was sweating as much as Yuri Modin was.

"We could request a meeting of Foreign Ministers," said Stalin, always stubborn.

"Comrade General Secretary, we may request it," said Yerofeyev, his voice was uncertain, though, "but we have to prepare for rejection."

Stalin lost his temper, rose from his seat, and tapped with his two fists on the desk.

"I want retaliatory measures," he yelled.

The people in the office were white and nailed in their seats, immobilized. Yerofeyev spoke first.

"We can organize a communist German state at our side," he whispered.

"Yes, we will create a new East German state from our side, I agree," acquiesced Stalin. He felt in part satisfied. "You will begin the negotiation, but try to obtain the Foreign Ministers meeting before the end of the blockade," he ordered.

"We will try, Comrade General Secretary," answered Yerofeyev.

When Stalin was alone in his study, he once again went to the window. He had lost and he did not like the feeling. The U.S. Air Force and the British RAF vanquished him. They were at the point of defeating the Supreme Soviet military, without bloodshed. He would find out who was the responsible for that defeat. He would purge once again those who failed to give a new victory to the Soviet Union.

Chapter 41
The Mission

John ran the 500 meters from the corner to the Eberhardt Villa with impatience in his heart. After two days of uninterrupted service, he had his one-day break. His only thoughts were of being with Esther, and they warmed his soul. These were the best moments in his life.

Esther waited him with the same impatience. Her kisses were long, warm, and breathtaking. Nevertheless, something was not right. Something strange was in the air and John got scared.

"What is the matter, Esther? Are you okay?"

"Of course."

She stepped backward and crossed her arms behind her back. John was alarmed. She always used that gesture when something important was happening to her.

"Hans Stolzer called me. It appears that the Soviets lowered the guard and we have the chance to pass through. We will depart in two days for Halle."

"What? Are you crazy? The blockade is not yet finished! This trip is foolish! Even in peacetime, it would be dangerous, and considering the present time, it is insane!"

"Do not tell that, John. We have already spoken about how important it is to me to find somebody from my family."

"That man is, in fact, not your family. He is an unknown uncle. He does not even know about you!"

"But I know about him; that is the fact, John."

John was pacing up and down in the small room. Esther was particularly calm. She knew that one day this crucial discussion would come. She sat in the armchair and looked at John with a serious expression. *He will understand; he just needs some more time.*

"Yes, you know about him, but why he is more important than our present life, the future we would have together? Why do you want to risk your own life for him?"

"John, I lost everybody I loved. My father, mother, my brother and sister are gone. My friends are gone. I did not find one living soul from my village. Nevertheless, I did find *him*. It is as though I found my family."

John was in despair. What he would be able to say? What could he say to hold her back?

"And John, I owe that to my grandfather…"

"What?"

"He was good to me, I will never forget his kindness, his patience, his strong belief in the future, I always wanted to be as him; as determined, as doubt-free. He wanted us to speak perfect German and that saved my life. I owe my life to him. I owe it to him to help his nephew."

"You owe it to him to stay alive! That's what you owe him!"

"And you John, you owe him me…"

"What?"

"Yes, John. You owe him me…. My grandfather brought home the English book. He found out how to build up inner resistance to the oppression by strengthening the mind. We learned English as response to the oppression, but today it received a new dimension. We are sitting here together, loving and cherishing each other, thanks to him, to his indestructible belief that open mind and open spirit are the real future in our world."

She went to John sitting on the edge of the bed, his face buried in his palms. She caressed his head lovingly, took his hands, and kissed them. She kneeled before him, and placed her beautiful face on his knees.

"You see, John, we are here today, together, thanks to him. You owe him me. You owe him to understand me and support my action. I need your loving support now." She pressed her cheek on his knee, smiling.

"It's only for a week. I will go in two days, and in one week we will be together once again."

182

John weakened. In her voice, he heard deep determination, and everything she said was beautiful and true. He was not able to fight it. He understood the only way was to go along with it. *She does love me, but she will never forget nor forgive if I do not follow her now,* he thought.

He rose and opened the window. The early spring sunshine was hot, but the fresh breeze was still cool. He took some deep breaths. He was looking to Esther. She was still sitting on the floor, her big green eyes wide opened, her face smiling. The sunshine illuminated her blonde hair. He knelt next to her and took her in his arms. He kissed her with all the tenderness in his heart.

"I love you. I want to have you alongside me all my life. Will you marry me, Esther?"

"Yes, I will, John. I love you with all my heart. My love will bring me back to you. You must believe it!"

Their solemn and everlasting embrace was the most beautiful moment of their lives.

Chapter 42
The Journey

The morning was cold and dark. The wind blew and spread the smell of spring. Esther did not think about the season this morning. She dressed fast and warm. She took the backpack she had prepared with care. Excitement filled her heart. Hans Stolzer arrived with the car at 4:30 exactly as planned. A half an hour later, they opened the door of the lounge in the restaurant, *Zum Schwarzen Wald*.

"Good morning, Esther!" Gerhard Sturm greeted his arriving friends. They shook hand and took the time to drink a cup of coffee. "Karl is ready and waiting for you, Esther."

The travelers, Esther, Karl and three other smugglers, passed through the little woods behind Tegel airport. Illegal passengers were unlikely here. The Soviets concentrated their efforts on the airport and lowered their vigilance elsewhere. The smugglers knew that, but they advanced with caution. They saw military guards twice, walking by, smoking their cigarettes. Esther was nervous. The others were calm and their calm reassured Esther.

They waited under the bushes. A minivan passed by and stopped for a moment. The travelers ran directly to the car and continued the trip to Potsdam. Arriving in Potsdam, they left the car and took the commuter bus. They arrived at the railway station of Potsdam at 9:00 A.M. when the express train from Magdeburg arrived. With their backpacks, they mingled among the passengers. The police officers did not verify departing passengers in the station, concentrating only on the incoming passengers. Berliners went to the countryside to exchange their belongings for more or less the same value in food. The police hunted the backpackers and confiscated all they could.

As planned, Esther's small group took their places in the overcrowded second-class car, with the destination Magdeburg. People were tired and silent. It was better, here in the Eastern zone, to keep your mouth shut and not say a word. One could never know who might be eavesdropping in the next seat. An agent could always be present. Esther felt relieved when the train arrived in Magdeburg.

The group dispersed in the railway station, choosing different paths to the harbor on the River Elbe. Esther stayed with Karl. The couple traveled by direct bus to the harbor. They crossed the downtown of Magdeburg. The gothic cathedral once rose across the Elbe River, but now it lay in ruins. The ruins of the war were still everywhere. They arrived at the barge at 6 P.M., ahead of schedule.

The river was the most secure method of transport for the smugglers. Police officers monitored traffic on the river only on rare occasion. The presence of police officers was more common in the harbors. Today, traffic was light; the wharf was deserted. Karl had a bad premonition. In general, they experienced more life here. He turned his attention to the departure, though.

The River Elbe meets the River Saale near to Magdeburg. On the Saale, the group would arrive directly at Halle without meeting anybody on the trip. Halle got its fame from salt production. From the middle age, handlers transported this precious salt on the river. Deliveries went far to the North to the big harbor cities along the North Sea. Halle was member of the Hanseatic League, thanks to its salt. For centuries, barge traffic remained untouched by any government.

The barge was uncomfortable. Esther was already tired. The thrill of the journey did not allow her to nap. Her spirit remained awake. She tried to sleep a bit, but the night was cold. She tightened her coat. They arrived at Halle before noon. The harbor was not deserted, but the usual crowd was missing as in Magdeburg. Karl once again had a strange feeling of premonition, but organizing the expedition became his primary concern.

The war caused major destruction to the region. The Messerschmidt aircraft factory occupied Leipzig, the nearby big town.

Allied bombs destroyed the region. Halle had some luck. By a miracle, the historical downtown stayed intact. The streetcar passed before the University building. The academy was the oldest University of Germany. At the main entrance, two lion statues adorned the elegant edifice that was built in late classicist style. The harmony of the complex impressed Esther. She did not intend to visit the town, though. She was impatient to arrive to the Mittelstrasse 11-13 and meet with her uncle, Avram Kohlberg.

When she knocked on the door in the backyard of the building in Mittelstrasse, her heart began to beat faster and her breathing was quicker. An old man opened the door. He was small, slim, and skinny, and an extraordinary sadness filled his eyes. Avram Kohlberg was fifty-eight years old, but appeared ten years older. He was surprised to see a beautiful young girl on the doorstep.

"Seit gesunt!" Esther greeted the man in Yiddish. The man was even more surprised to hear the Yiddish words.

"Seit gesunt!" he whispered with an uncertain voice.

"Are you Avram Kohlberg? I am looking for Avram Kohlberg. Do you know him?"

"Yes, I am he," said the old man, astonished.

"My name is Esther Kohlberg."

Avram Kohlberg felt as though the world was collapsing around him. He was close to passing out.

"May I come in?" asked Esther.

"Oh, yes, of course. Excuse me."

The furniture of the apartment was simple and functional. An old grand piano stood in the corner giving to the living room an artistic atmosphere. Esther sat in one of the armchairs. Avram Kohlberg was still in shock. He did not know who this young girl was, but her name was the same as his. Memories and feelings were rushing in his head and in his heart.

"Avram, I am your niece. My grandfather came from Halle. Perhaps, you remember the family history and you have heard of him. I am a survivor of the death camp, Treblinka. When I was looking for my relatives, I received your address through the Red Cross."

Avram Kohlberg was staring at Esther. Yes, he remembered the family legend. He heard about the Kohlberg family in Ukraine and the distant Rabin. The family did not forget him. Tears came in his eyes. Family? *Where is the family now?* He lost his whole family. His wife, Rosa, committed suicide in *Trauerhalle* on the eve of their deportation to Buchenwald. God spared her the suffering in the camp.

"They are gone, Esther... they are all gone."

Avram Kohlberg buried his face in his hands, crying like a child. Esther rose and went to him. She had also tears in the eyes. She knew the meaning of each tear. She embraced the old man and they stayed there a while. Esther wiped the tears and broke the silence.

"Avram, I came from West Berlin. I know the Soviets. You will not find freedom here, or understanding either. I came for you. Come with me! We will go back together to West Berlin, and from there to West Germany."

"Do you want me to leave Halle?"

"Yes. What do you have in Halle? You have only memories."

"I am an old man, Esther..."

"It is never too late to live free, Avram. We have nobody left. We have each other now. That will be our Kohlberg family."

Avram Kohlberg rose and went to the piano. He was a musician, a piano accordionist and a piano shopkeeper in Halle. He played some notes on the keys, and showed a sad smile on his face.

"You see, I will never play again. My hands are no longer good for the piano..." He caressed the music instrument tenderly. "I suppose, I have to abandon it here."

"Yes, Avram. We have to leave at once. You can have a backpack. I have people who will help us to pass through the border to the French sector in Berlin."

"Once again, I have to run off with all my possessions on my back."

"This time, Avram, you go for the freedom and for a better life."

Avram Kohlberg gazed at the young girl who was his niece. He did not even know about her one hour ago. He felt life is coming back to him. She was enthusiastic, positive and convincing.

Fifty-eight is not so old... He would cling on life. She was right. He had to go with her.

Avram Kohlberg was ready within an hour. Fear and excitement filled his heart. The arrival of Esther changed his life. All of a sudden, he found a relative to share the feeling of family loss. He felt relieved, and courageous. His travel with Esther would be their exodus toward a better life. As they left the apartment, Avram carefully closed the door. Taking a deep breath, he looked into the eyes of Esther, and left the building without turning back.

When they crossed the market place of Halle, Avram stopped a moment in front of the statue of Händel. The great German composer was born in Halle. The nine-foot-high statue in bronze on a marble pedestal dominated the place. Turning toward his second home, England, the statue represented Georg Friedrich Händel conducting his Messiah. Avram adored his sparkling baroque music. While he heard in his spirit the well-known musical notes, he did not notice the car passing with high speed in the street. He jumped away from it in the last moment.

The car stopped two blocks from them and the officer from the back seat entered the building of the Soviet military administration, in a hurry. Captain Schulz had received orders to appear at once in the office of the political commissar. He was nervous. The orders were mysterious. Who could know what would happen in the next moment in these days? He waited with impatience and fear in the outer office.

The political commissar hung up the phone with his superior. Last year, the Soviet communication services dismantled the telephone lines crossing through the Western sectors of Berlin. During fourteen days, long distance phone calls were impossible. When the Soviets restored the connection, they passed the lines through a Soviet center. The permanent supervision of long distance communication provided highly valuable information to them. The last developments alarmed the Soviet Administration.

The Soviet officers agreed on the necessity of exemplary actions. The political commissar once again analyzed the information held in the folder on his desk before calling the local police officer. When the

German Captain entered the office, he had the most serious expression on his face.

"Comrade Schulz, that is an urgent matter!" said the Commissar. "Black market activities and the smuggling in this town have been going on unpunished for a long time. We request immediate action!"

"Comrade Commissar, according to our previous meeting, we ignored these activities because we needed them to provide merchandise and goods not available to us in any other way!"

"I know that, Comrade, but read these reports I received a moment ago. You will understand..." The Commissar handed over the folder on his desk to Captain Schulz. When Captain Schulz read the information, he became white. "This is indeed troublesome."

"As you see Comrade Schulz, the organization is ready now to pass people through the border. We cannot allow that. Today, they will pass one person and tomorrow the whole nation will go away."

"Yes, I agree, Comrade Commissar."

"We have to stop them here and now, for we do not want to set up an ambush too close to Berlin. We have to avoid international complications."

"Yes, Comrade Commissar! We will take care of that at once!"

"Wait a minute! Do it carefully! It is in our best interest to obtain more information!"

"Yes, Comrade Commissar."

As soon as he arrived to the police headquarters, Captain Schulz organized an assault team composed of well-trained German police officers armed up to the teeth, and thus prepared for any eventuality. They had watched the organization at the harbor for several months. They knew where to go. The police cars stopped three blocks away from the Hafenstrasse. The majority of the police officers were in civilian clothing. A team in regular uniform backed up the operations, waiting for a signal.

Karl organized the last step to load the barge. He looked nervously at his watch. Esther should have been here a half an hour ago. The bad premonition accompanied him all the day. He pressed to speed up the departure. When Esther entered the warehouse with the old man, Karl was relieved. They were able to hurry now.

The quay was empty. Everything appeared calm. Esther and Avram waited at the back door. They were ready. All of a sudden, the smugglers became alert.

"I saw police cars in the neighborhood!" said one of them to Karl. "We have to hurry! They are preparing something!"

The premonition grew to the certainty of disaster in Karl's mind. He had to take care of Esther and Avram; Gerhard would hold him responsible.

"Esther, you will go here. You have to walk slowly to the barge. We will cover you."

Esther was certain everything would be in order. She smiled at Avram and motioned to him as she opened the back door. They stepped out into the shadows of the evening, crossing the quay slowly as normal pedestrians would do. At that moment, they heard gunfire. Startled, they stopped and looked back, and they stared at one other.

At the first gunfire, police rushed out from the shadows of the buildings. Esther and Avram did not realize what was happening. Karl rushed to the back door. Esther turned back and saw him. The shooting was widespread. Karl hurried to the corner and signaled Esther to run to the barge. Esther turned back to Avram. At that moment, Karl heard the yell. He turned back and saw Esther collapse. Avram fell on the knees and held Esther in his arms.

Karl stopped for a moment. From the shadows, he saw the police officers encircle Esther and Avram. A car stopped beside them. He was not able to see what happened to them. He had to run. He by-passed the warehouse and succeeded in catching the car they used in Halle. He picked up another smuggler two blocks further. When he took his place on the express train in the Magdeburg railway station three hours later, he was still not able to believe what had happened. He buried his face in his hands. Esther was lost. He was not in the position to do anything for her. He hoped Gerhard and Hans would understand. Once again, the innocents were paying the price of history.

Chapter 43
Lost Happiness

John jumped from the pilot's seat and with hasty steps headed to Tom Crawley's office. Esther left a week ago and every moment he waited her return. His impatience increased every day.

Tom Crawley smoked his cigar at the window, his hands in his pockets. He was submerged in his thoughts. He barely heard John entering the office. He turned slowly and fixed his gaze on the young man.

"Hi Tom. What's up old, chap? What — " John interrupted what he was about to ask when he saw Hans Stolzer standing in the corner. He felt suddenly chilled. *Something happened to Esther;* he felt it clear in the pit of his stomach...

"Esther — What has happened to Esther?"

"We do not know for sure, John," said Hans, gravely. "Everything was gone as planned, but in Halle, on the return trip the KGB made a raid and our men got caught. There was a lot of shouting and gunfire. The KGB arrested many of them and some were killed."

"And Esther? What about her?"

"At best, she was with the arrested persons. Nevertheless, it is possible she had suffered severe wounds. We do not have any more information. Our contact is broken with the local organization."

John felt the world collapse around him. He would prefer to be a boy and let his tears come flooding down, but he was a veteran war pilot, an adult man and he had to be strong in front of these strong men. He did not want to accept the evidence he knew in his heart. In his head, he also knew: it is over. Esther was in the Soviets' hands, perhaps hurt, or possibly dead. He would not be able to make that go away.

"Tom, is there a possibility that we can do something? The military has to be able to find a way and bring her out somehow! What do you think?"

"I do not know, John. You may try... We could give a try... Let's go right now to Military Intelligence. I will get a meeting with officials in the mayor's office, and perhaps they are in the position to help in getting a diplomatic solution. We will exhaust all the possibilities..."

"Tom, I want to try everything..."

The military intelligence officer listened to them carefully, noting every detail. He promised to try obtaining information. He made it clear though, the situation did not look favorable.

The mayor's office was sorry about the loss of Esther. The associates in the office knew her well; they worked close together. Her enthusiasm, good humor, and outgoing and optimistic personality gained her much support. They were not able though to do anything to help her and John for all intents and purposes. They had limited links with the other side behind the Brandenburg Gate.

In the coming days, John spent all his time organizing meetings and campaigns designed to free Esther, but without success. Things got even worse.

Despite despising Gerhard Sturm, he met with him. John never liked the man with his superior Aryan air, or his having influence from the money he earned in the black market. Now, personal differences were secondary. According to new information, Esther had serious wounds. If she survived the injuries, the KGB would transport her to a military hospital where she would be under KGB surveillance. She had little chance to survive a KGB prison camp.

John still refused to give up.

Two weeks later, the Soviets lifted the blockade. West Berlin remained free. Faced with determination and financial and technological power, the Soviets had no other choice but to retreat. The Berliners' determination and tenacity created an island in the heart of the most important Soviet ally. West Berlin would keep standing, independent, courageous and prospering.

John was walking the well-known street alone. The crowd surrounded him, celebrating, happy, and proud. Unknown citizens hugged the American soldier, tapped him on his shoulder or saluted him with friendship and with thankfulness. The citizens of West Berlin knew that without the American determination, their city would not have won out in this contest of political wills.

John's thoughts turned to the moment when he passed here in the company of Esther. He had a meeting with General Clay. Despite of General Clay's tremendous influence, he was not able to promise anything to the young pilot. Moreover, he was leaving West Berlin.

Berliners organized a touching celebration for the end of the blockade and the farewell of General Clay. The joyful crowd filled the big square at the City Hall. Mayor Ernst Reuter was the first to step on the stand.

"The attempt to force us to our knees has failed, frustrated by our steadfastness and firmness. It failed because the world heard our appeal and came to our assistance. Berlin will always remain Berlin."

That historic statement sentence generated an outstanding ovation. Ernst Reuter remembered the General in his words.

"General Clay entered Berlin as a victor. He will leave as our friend."

Thousands and thousands of participants applauded with warm heart. They were here, at the celebration, to say goodbye to General Clay. The disciplined soldier had tears in his eyes when he took the microphone.

"There are two classes of airlift heroes: first, the pilots, who flew the planes to Berlin in every kind of weather; and secondly, the people of Berlin who, after choosing freedom, were also prepared to make the necessary sacrifices to uphold it."

John listened to the orators, but he did not hear the words. He felt his heart bound in cold ropes. The surrounding happiness did not touch him. For him everything was lost. Esther was lost; their happiness was lost. The Soviets lifted the blockade, but the Iron Curtain had definitely fallen on Eastern Europe.

The Soviets exploded their A-bomb in August 1949. From now on, the world would engage in a permanent struggle between war and peace, between total destruction and survival. John knew that no workable relationship would be possible between the two blocks.

John found himself in front of Brandenburg Gate. The elegant architecture, once in the middle of one of the cultural centers of Europe, now symbolized the separation between two worlds. The sunset gave a golden aura to the statues. John held his gaze at the beautiful image of that magic sunset, and knew his life would never be the same.

PART V.

MORE POSTCARDS FROM THE PAST

Chapter 44
West Berlin, 1989

The taxi by-passed the Siegessäule, the pillar of victory and turned toward the Zoo in the downtown of West Berlin. Traffic was heavy at this time of the day and the taxi stopped at the red light. John Carpenter in the backseat noticed the Brandenburg Gate at the end of the main boulevard. The setting sun shined on the statues on the top of it with the red flag still beside them. He studied the well-known architecture. Disordered thoughts came across his mind.

When the plane landed on Tegel Airport, he could not breathe because of his tension. He did not recognize the airport, now modern, international, and crowded. Tegel airport was no different from any airport located in the large metro centers of the world. He recalled images of the military airport facility forty years ago, now a dazzling place filled with sparkling life.

The taxi continued straight in the Klingelhöferstrasse, turned left into the Lützowufer and stopped before the Grand Hotel Esplanade. The white L-shaped building dominated the quay. The war destroyed the original building where Greta Garbo once resided during her stay in Berlin. Today, this reconstructed building glittered in all its past glamour. A bellman ran to the taxi and took care of the luggage. John Carpenter entered the lobby. The old Berlin, still present in his mind, no longer existed. He felt as though he was in a dream. The new generation did not know about the past suffering existing only in his memory. Life took over and this solemn impression was marvelous. He smiled when he entered his room adorned in art-deco style.

He wanted to have a nap, but fatigue and the excitement did not let him sleep. He was sipping a whisky when the phone rang.

Peter Slauter, the young military intelligence officer was in the lobby. He could not wait to meet with John and draw up the action plan for the coming weeks.

"Hello! How was the trip? Are you satisfied with the hotel? Do you want to have dinner?"

"Yes to both; yes, the trip was comfortable, however long and yes, a good dinner will be welcome."

They left the hotel and took a walk on Kurfürststrasse, the popular center of West Berlin. The warm summer weather tempted the Berliners, and the street was full. They chose a Kneipe, a traditional German pub. John wanted something typical, sour cabbage with sausage. He had eaten that often forty years ago.

Peter Slauter had already made up a program and wanted to obtain John's approval. He spoke enthusiastically.

"I organized a meeting with the Consular Section of the U.S. Embassy here in West Berlin. We have to coordinate our action plan with the Intelligence Office. You will need a valid visa for the countries in the region."

John nodded. Peter's professional approach was reassuring; he had to admit.

"On the other hand, Peter, I will need an interpreter. Would you find somebody for me? Perhaps a student?" suggested John.

"Yes, of course! I will propose somebody for you! Let me check with her."

"That is perfect, Peter! I am looking forward to it."

The dinner was excellent. The warm weather cooled down for this late hour. Peter left John in front of the hotel, but John needed some exercise. His jet lag would not let him sleep. He walked around the hotel. His steps led him toward an unknown destination. All of a sudden, he realized he was facing the Wall on Potsdamer Platz. The deserted square was sinister. Big reflectors illuminated the gray concrete wall. He had never seen the Wall; the East German government built it in 1961, long after he left West Berlin.

When the East German government completely and definitely closed the border in 1952, the unique remaining way to escape to the West was Berlin. Many East German citizens went to Berlin, bought a suburban train or a subway ticket and left East Berlin despite the closed crossing points and controls at the border. Between 1949 and 1961, more than 2.6 million East Germans escaped to West Berlin, when the total population of East Germany was about seventeen million. On August 13, 1961, the East German government built up the Wall in one night. Only two weeks later, the East German border guard shot Günter Litwin, the first victim of the Wall. During the decades, five thousands East Germans attempted to escape at the Wall.

John was gazing to it and sadness filled his heart. He knew about the Wall, but experiencing it before his eyes was different. The Wall expressed all the hopelessness, desperation, and misery that an entire nation and whole Eastern Europe behind the Iron Curtain endured for decades. His mission became more important than ever.

After returning to his hotel room, he switched on the television. He looked for an American broadcast channel and chose CNN. Astonished, he saw tanks rolling over the students on Tiananmen Square in Beijing. Once again, a totalitarian regime gripped weapons against non-armed students to stop a movement for democracy and freedom. What destiny would be waiting for the people of Eastern Europe?

He was still in his thoughts when, next day, he took the taxi to the Consular Section of the U.S. Embassy in Berlin.

"Clayallee 170, *bitte schön!*"

Giving that address brought warmness to his heart. In addition, he noticed the Consular Section was in front of the Truman Plaza complex. Memory of the Americans playing a decisive role in the event forty years ago was present in the town. John felt comfortable.

The Consular Section was in turmoil. The tragic incidents in Beijing motivated the overall stress. The Chief Intelligence Officer received John and Peter in the small conference room. The debriefing was short, but detailed.

"Gentlemen! Let us go over the timetable of this year, 1989, concentrating on Eastern Europe! Be in Czechoslovakia, Poland, Hungary, or Lithuania, thousands and thousands were demonstrating for freedom and democracy. As a result, the introduction of multi-party systems and organizations of free election are a reality."

Peter Slauter took over from the Chief Officer.

"The events on Tiananmen Square tend to counteract all these positive development," he said.

The Chief Intelligence Officer had concerns about the East German political situation.

"That is true, Peter. Using the force of weapons could also tempt the East German political circles in an easy way. We have to add to the analysis that the East German authorities do not seem to alter their politics. In February, the guard shot the twenty-year old Chris Gueffroy, while he attempted to escape through the Wall. The total number of deaths at the Wall amounts now to two hundred and thirty nine. In addition, in April at the Chausseestrasse, border guards' gunfire stopped two teenagers trying to escape."

The room was stilled in silence. Peter broke the stillness.

"In my point of view, the main issue at that moment is Hungary. Regarding the situation of the East German escapees in Hungary, the East German government is pressing for immediate and decisive action to expel their escaped citizens from Hungary."

The Chief Officer nodded. Peter Slauter felt encouraged to continue.

"Perhaps, you do not know, John, but Hungary was in Honecker's bad books in the last years. East Germans needed a travel authorization to that country. This year, an incredible number of East Germans defected to Hungary. They are staying in Hungary in escapees' camps, many of them near to the Austrian border."

"Yes, we heard that reported on television," nodded John. His attention turned toward the situation. "We heard also that the Hungarians dismantled the barbed wires at their Western borders with Austria."

"That is the most amazing event of these last years!" Peter Slauter chimed in enthusiastically. "Mister Gorbachev's politics resulted in direct and independent action in the satellite countries. In addition, the Hungarian opposition groups are organizing a Pan-European Picnic near to the Austrian border during their national holiday in August."

"Let me add," said the Chief Intelligence Officer, "that President Bush arrives to Budapest in the coming weeks. The turmoil in the region will dominate his visit. This presidential visit will fortify, however, the forces of freedom and will boost movements for democracy. That is our hope, and I am sure it is the will of the President."

"As an observer, I want to be the closest possible to the events. Would you be able to organize a trip to Hungary for me?" asked John.

The Chief Intelligence Officer agreed and ordered Peter to carry out the necessary preparations.

"Of course! In a week we should be ready to fly to Hungary."

"We, did you say?" asked John, smiling.

"Yes, I will come to help you in dealing with the U.S. Embassy in Budapest," said Peter.

While waiting for the official papers, John enjoyed visiting Tempelhof airport. Nostalgia gripped his heart. With touching feeling, he stood in front of the Airlift Memorial. Indeed, the Berliners did not forget. He looked forward to the mission directing him once again into a troubled region of Europe.

Chapter 45
In Budapest

Ambassador Palmer energetically supervised the work in front of the U.S. Embassy in Budapest on Szabadság Square. He was proud to revive the memory of the courageous Brigadier General Harry Hill Brandholtz who was Provost Marshall to General Pershing at the end of World War I. He arrived to Hungary in August 1919 to oversee the disengagement of Romanian troops from Hungary. On October 5, 1919, a group of Romanian soldiers entered the Hungarian National Museum and attempted to remove the Transylvanian treasures. As head of the American Military Mission, the General, armed only with a riding crop, stopped them with a bluff. The grateful Hungarians erected his statue in 1936, but the communist regime took it away "for repairs" in the late forties. The former Ambassador, Mister Salgo, placed it in the gardens of his official residence. Ambassador Palmer obtained permission to re-install the statue in Szabadság Square at its original location.

Ambassador Palmer was agitated. President Bush would arrive in a few days. The statue's reinstatement was part of the official program symbolizing warming of the relationship between the United States and Hungary. President Bush would arrive in an amazing period and the Ambassador was especially anxious about organization. The presidential visit would take place only some weeks after the ceremony, at Heroes' Square, for the reburial of Imre Nagy, the executed leader of the Hungarian Revolution in 1956. A crowd of a quarter of million people attended the solemn ceremony. When the Soviet tanks rolled over the unarmed people in 1956, the reform communist took shelter in the Embassy of Yugoslavia where he had been offered protection. Under promise of safe passage, he left the embassy, but the Yugoslav bus was seized by the Soviet military.

202

Nagy was held prisoner for approximately two years. After a secret trial, Nagy was executed in 1958.

The attention of Ambassador Palmer turned toward the classical building behind him. The religious leader, Cardinal Mindszenty, made a better decision in 1956 when he requested asylum at the U.S. Embassy. On November 4, 1956, the Air Attaché, Colonel Welwyn Dallam, a Marine Corporal, and the Master Sergeant were standing on the stairs at the entrance to the Chancery. Cardinal Mindszenty and a Monsignor walked to the door. They asked to come into the U.S. Embassy. The American guards looked at each other, but the Air Attaché nodded. The Corporal unlocked the door and Cardinal Mindszenty walked in. A few moments later, a telex arrived from Washington instructing the Embassy to extend every courtesy, should the Cardinal request asylum.

The Cardinal stayed in the Embassy for fifteen years. He used what is now the Ambassador's office as his salon and he slept in the other, smaller room to the side. Embassy officers brought him food and reading material, walked with him in the Embassy courtyard and attended Mass with him. The police outside of the Chancery were ever watchful should he try to escape. They ran their engines day and night, twenty-four hours a day, seven days a week, prepared for all eventualities. The CIA and the American Intelligence showed their strength, when on September 28, 1971, they succeeded in smuggling the Cardinal out of the building and transporting him to the United States under the eyes of the communist watchdogs. Ambassador Palmer smiled. Everyday, when he entered his office, he had to remember the Cardinal.

Ambassador Palmer walked back to the building with abrupt steps. He had to organize and manage the presidential visit. On the top of it, he had to find time for the visitors from West Berlin. The meeting would be short. The participants were waiting for him in the small conference room. The Ambassador knew Peter Slauter, and welcomed him. The Consular Secretary joined the group.

"Gentlemen!" began the Ambassador, "As you imagine, the visit of President Bush is a major event in the relationship between the

United States and Hungary. This visit takes place in a hot and bothered moment. Rehabilitation of the 1956's revolutionaries and the dismantlement of the barbed wire at the Hungarian-Austrian border drained the fury of the conventional communist leaders toward Hungary, as you were able to experience it in East Germany. For the moment, Moscow is watching in silence."

"President Bush makes a courageous step visiting the East European countries in this particular moment!" said John, impressed by the political influence of the presidential visit. "His presence in these controversial countries underlines the American involvement in the democratic transformation of the region."

"You are right," nodded the Ambassador acknowledging John's precise remark. "This visit will fortify, for sure, the supporters of transformation. You will observe the popular support coming from the Hungarian people. You are more than welcome to attend the different programs of the visit."

"Thank you!" answered John and Peter at the same time.

The Consular Secretary was silent until up that moment. He felt that his intervention became necessary.

"In the coming days before the visit of President Bush, I would like, however, to advise you to inquire about the coming Pan-European Picnic in August. The organizers of this long-planned demonstration obtained the patronage of Mister Otto von Habsburg and Mister Imre Pozsgay, Hungary's most reform-minded communist."

"It is interesting to hear that," said Peter. "The Habsburg royal family dominated the Hungarian political life for centuries. They crushed all revolutions and wars of independence directed against them. If I understand accurately, is the Habsburg family in fact backing a movement in common with communists?"

"Yes, that is the situation," answered the Consular Secretary. "I too, found it curious, but that is the case. Otto von Habsburg is eminent figure in the Pan-European movement and member in the European Parliament. Setting aside the curiosity of the situation, I think, however, it is important that a large common front is backing the reforms and the democratic changes in the region. For that reason, I would like to suggest that you investigate this organization."

"Thank you for the information," answered John. "I can assure you, we will follow up with that issue."

The information filled the minds of Peter and John. To refresh their heads, John proposed to walk back to the hotel instead of taking the subway. The Chancery Building of the U.S. Embassy was a block away from the Danube on the Pest side. The majestic Danube flows in the middle of the city, between Pest and Buda. The Buda hills drop sharply into the river, and the entirely flat Pest sits on the opposite bank.

The walk led Peter and John to the Parliament Building near the Embassy. The Hungarian Parliament is the most imposing Parliament in Central Europe. An immense cupola divided the two symmetric aisles. The size, the rhythm, and the harmony of the complex, built in neo-gothic style, left John breathless. Continuing on the border walk, the view was even more spectacular. Castle Hill in front of them, on the opposite side of the river appeared in its entire baroque splendor. The tourist cruise ships and waterbuses on the Danube River enriched the idyllic landscape. John felt as though he was in the middle of a story. The impressive river with the large waterfront in the middle of a metropolis was unique. The smell of water refreshed the hot summer air. In the late afternoon, the lighted Chain Bridge connecting the two banks of the river appeared as million fireflies. The walkway leading to their Hotel Intercontinental, the American hotel in Budapest, was filled with Budapestians mingling among the tourists. The downtown, including the pedestrian precinct crowded with shops, coffeehouses, and restaurants had a pleasant, sparkling atmosphere. The terraces of the cafés were busy with guests. *Budapest is as Paris. Yes, it is the Paris of the East,* thought John. Collected information whirled in his head, but the walk of the afternoon helped him to have a good sleep. *Tomorrow will be an excellent day.*

Chapter 46
The Presidential Visit

A standing ovation welcomed President Bush in the big auditorium of the Karl Marx University in Budapest. His visit generated overwhelming enthusiasm among the Hungarian people. They greeted, celebrated, and accompanied him with signs of friendship coming from their hearts.

While he was walking through the large halls of the University, images and emotions of the day before were still on his mind. He thought they would stay engraved in his memory forever. At the Austrian border, he received a piece of the Iron Curtain that had been dismantled in the months before his visit. When he took the piece of barbed wire in his hands, tears came in his eyes. This was a piece of history, that he held in his hands, representing forty years of struggling, resisting and striving of an entire region of Europe.

"We believe that the artificial, physical, and spiritual wall still existing in the world some day shall collapse everywhere," said the President with trembling voice. "This is truly beautiful. Thank you, all of you!"

He realized at that moment, how important his visit was. His presence would boost the supporters of democracy, and help the circle of political reformers speed up economic transformations. The presidential visit expressed American determination to help the revolution in Eastern Europe to succeed smoothly and without bloodshed.

President Bush entered the big auditorium of the University. Smiling, he stepped onto the stand and greeted the audience with a wave. His eyes ran all over the people in the auditorium. The audience consisted of participants of the Hungarian political and economical life, but the overwhelming majority was young students. The Karl Marx University was the Harvard Business School of Hungary. The future leaders of the Hungarian political and economical landscape were sitting in the room and their eyes fixed on the American president.

President Bush spoke on political and economic reforms. In his delegation, eminent figures from large American companies took part. The President announced a series of steps designated to further demonstrate the U.S. support for ongoing reforms in Hungary. In the crowd, John Carpenter listened to the President. He did never hope to approach the President of the United States so close. He was proud.

John could not control his own emotion. He felt an electric charge going through the atmosphere in the big auditorium of the University. At the same time, the historical impact of that visit amazed him. The communist hardliners would fail in their attempt to stop the march of history. In that conviction, the overall enthusiasm carried him away.

John's mission developed successfully in establishing connections and relationships with the different groups of the Hungarian opposition. Following the advice of the Consular Secretary, he directed his attention to the organization of that Pan-European Picnic. Peter introduced him to a photojournalist, Thomas Lobenwein. Returning to Berlin, Peter Slauter left John in the hands of his journalist friend, who was happy to guide John around in Budapest and in Hungary.

John's interest turned toward the East German refugees. The Hungarian authorities accommodated all those having their travel documents expired and that refused to return in East Germany in refugee camp. The most important installation was in Budapest, in the district of Zugliget. Zugliget, "the hidden garden" was a popular hiking paradise in the Buda Hills. When John and Thomas entered the camp, it was bubbling with excitement.

The reason for the excitement was new information circulating about the Pan-European Picnic. John gazed with astonishment to the flyer in his hand. He did not expect to find such information on a flyer in an East-German refugee camp. *What was happening here? How did all these people know about that picnic?* He wanted to know more about that and these refugees were better informed than he was. Many of the refugees had family in West Germany and they received phone calls and letters. West German TV stations broadcasted steady reportages on the organization. The importance of the picnic grew in the eyes of John.

"Thomas," he asked the reporter, "where this picnic will take place?"

"In a small border village called Sopronpuszta," answered Thomas. "Today, the major part of the barbed wire on the Austrian border is dismantled. During the Hungarian National Holiday, the opposition groups are organizing this picnic on August 19, 1989, in this small village, where an old gate equipped with barbed wires still exists. During the celebration, they will open the gate and the participants will walk to the next small village, St. Margareth, in Austria. The political gathering at the foot of the Iron Curtain is an utmost courageous step. It will symbolize the opening of a new era in East-West relations. At least, the organizers and we, Hungarians, all hope for that."

"I already heard about the Pan-European Picnic," responded John. "I would like to make a trip there. Would you help me, Thomas?"

"Of course!" said the journalist, enthusiastically. "I am from Sopron, the nearest city to the event location! I would be more than happy to guide you there."

When they arrived in Sopron, John sensed something special in the air. History was marching and he was part of it.

Chapter 47
The Breakthrough

The grandiose music notes of the organ filled the Evangelist Church in Sopron. The organ concerts held on a regular basis attracted many guests present in the town. In addition to the national holiday celebration, the upcoming Pan-European Picnic attracted reporters from all over the world. Representatives of broadcasting companies, TV stations and newspapers, along with political celebrities, occupied the hotels of Sopron and surrounding region.

John Carpenter marveled at the toccatas and fugues by Johann Sebastian Bach. The artist at the organ was excellent. John's eyes ran all over the gilded wooden altar and the carved pulpit, main decorations of the Church. His spirit was flying with the rhythm of the music and the happenings of the last days. Sopron literally charmed him. The small town was a living museum. The Roman settlement, Scrabantia, was still present in the center of town. The baroque, gothic, and renaissance monuments along with medieval elements comprised the downtown of Sopron. The thousand-year old Hungarian History was smiling on him through the curving streets and artistic atmosphere.

The richness of the baroque music was still vibrating in John's head, when next day, ahead of schedule, he arrived to Sopronpuszta. The Pan-European Picnic would take place in the afternoon, but John wanted to be part of the preparations. He wanted to observe the people. He was astonished. Popularity of the event exceeded by far the forecast of the organizers. The rainstorm of the previous day transformed the meadows into muddy field. Parking was not possible there and cars were stationed all along the connecting roadsides. John was amazed to see so many cars with East German license numbers.

The Hungarian policemen and border guards concentrated on the old gate and barbed-wire fence, where the celebration and the symbolical opening were to take place some hours later. On the other side of the fence, the inhabitants of St. Margareth were gathering also. The mayor of St. Margareth, Andreas Waha, was among the participants. Onlookers took places in the trees, on pillars and fences. A strange premonition struck John. Something extraordinary was happening before his eyes. He was not able to put his feelings into words.

The commander of the Hungarian border guards, István Róka, was upset. The crowd increased by the minute. He received information that a large number of East German refugees were nearing to the border. He tried to maintain detached supervision.

All of a sudden, John noticed people leaving the central crowd and walking in line in the direction of the border. They were East Germans, their faces dark, tired, and determined. They were fathers and mothers; they were families and single persons; they were young and elderly; they were children and parents; they were men and women. John was surprised. He had difficulty in finding his way to come here, but these people knew where to go. His visit some days ago in the refugee camp came to mind. He remembered the flyers. His attention turned entirely toward this group of people. He understood something important was happening.

István Róka and the border guards were confused. The people nearing to the border were not wearing white shirts and pressed pants. These people were weary, exhausted, injured and worn-out. The border guards did not understand what was happening.

Several lines of East German refugees gathered to form a block at the border. The determined group acted, by all appearances, according to a plan. Hunky young men led the group, while women and children marched in the middle of the block. All of a sudden, the meandering block stopped in front of the gate, and closed their ranks. John heard a yell, a sharp order. At that moment, the group, with all the force of determined human beings, pressed themselves against the fence. The old gate was not able to resist. Chains and locks broke away and the East German refugees forced their way into Austria.

The border guards were armed, but Commander István Róka did not give order to fire. They could not act according their orders. Any gunshot would create carnage.

The refugees spread out at the border. In the tumult, a young mother holding his child in her arms stumbled and the child fell out of her arms. The running people did not notice the child. An alert Hungarian border guard did. He took the child in his arms and handed him over to the mother. He motioned her to run toward the opened gate. She stopped for a moment, turned and smiled at the guard, and ran away.

John absorbed the beauty of the moment. He looked to the other side of the border. The East Germans stopped, returned, and beckoned the others. They were free. It was the beginning of a new life.

In a few hours, almost seven hundred refugees surged joyfully through the border gate. Once across, the East Germans kept going. The Austrian gendarmes ferried them to a meeting point and fed them. Afterward, a fleet of buses, chartered in advance by the West Germans, took them to the West German Embassy in Vienna, where British and French diplomats helped issue them with the necessary papers. That was the new European cooperation.

In the next few days, fifteen thousand East German refugees would cross the Hungarian border to Austria. The East German government's protest was immediate.

John took the plane to West Berlin. He had to concentrate on the communist reaction. When the plane took off from Ferihegy, the airport of Budapest, he looked down on the Hungarian capital. The Hungarians had started something formidable. He was proud to witness a unique moment of history.

Chapter 48
The Interpreter

John arranged his tie and vest. His eyes fell on the folder placed on the desk. He opened it once again. The information was important, but not surprising.

East Germany protested to Hungary with anger, demanding that Hungary closes its border and ends the exodus to freedom for thousands. In the last days, the war of words intensified when the Soviet Union also added its condemnation. The East German communists considered Hungary's behavior to be a clear violation of legal treaties, against the basic interests of the East German state. At the same time, Yegor Ligachev, one of the leading hardliners in the Kremlin, arrived in East Berlin. Despite the Soviet claims that it was a visit to discuss agricultural problems, Western diplomats had no doubt that his main purpose was a crisis talk with East Germany's Communist Party chiefs. The crisis increased every day.

East German citizens, excited by the enthusiasm about the exodus at the Hungarian border, began to flow to Czechoslovakia. Czechoslovakia was the unique travel destination still authorized for them by the communist regime. All of a sudden, thousands of East German citizens took the West German Embassy in Prague under siege. *What would be their destiny?* Diplomatic chaos reigned in Europe. The meeting of the hardliners put a question mark on the immediate future.

John put the folder back on the desk. He was not satisfied with himself. Despite his obvious accomplishments, he was not comfortable in his role. He needed his own interpreter. He wanted to go to Prague. The events of the last days without doubt indicated, his place as observer is in Prague. The interpreter would help him to act on his own. Peter Slauter promised him an interpreter, his girlfriend from Israel, a linguistic student at the University of West Berlin.

He looked at the old pocket watch in his hand. It was time to go to the lobby and meet Peter and the young girl who would be his interpreter for the coming weeks.

The young people were waiting for him. Peter's tall figure dominated the lobby. The girl stayed in front of Peter and John was not able to see her face. The way Peter looked at the young woman gave John the idea that this girl meant more to Peter, than just a friend who happened to be female.

All of a sudden, John heard the girl's musical laugh. He stopped as though frozen. In his memory, a particular jingling laugh came alive. He heard this familiar sound forty years ago! He composed himself. The last days and weeks revived the old memories and now these memories were playing jokes with his imagination.

"Hi John! Let me introduce Edith Fischer."

"How do you do, Mister Carpenter? I'm glad to meet you and even more, I'm delighted to be your interpreter."

"Hello, Miss Fischer. The pleasure is mine."

John did not believe his eyes. Under the short shiny gold hair with a hint of red glimmer, a pair of big green eyes was gazing at him. Life was spinning him in circles. Memories were flooding in his mind and he had difficulty in concentrating. He was hoping that the others did not recognize his emotions.

He was up late that night; sleep did not come easy. Memories of Esther confused him. He did not want to believe that there could be a connection between Esther and Edith, but he was determined to find out.

Chapter 49
The Train

"This is unbelievable! I am extremely proud to be here," said Edith, enthusiastically. The day's experience at the Embassy of West Germany stimulated her. John smiled. The fire of the young woman was encouraging. He shared her amazement.

Refugees overwhelmed the West German Embassy of Prague. This afternoon, at the time of their visit, around four thousand East German citizens crowded together in the gardens. Their numbers increased daily. When East Germany blocked travel to Hungary, the fleeing East Germans turned to Czechoslovakia and gathered at the West German Embassy in Prague. John and Edith knew that, but experiencing the reality of it was different. Despair and determination radiated from the eyes of the homeless occupants of the embassy grounds.

These men and women had no prospects, no future, and no illusions. They wanted a better life for their children. Their requests were much more than the simple right to travel. Edith noticed a couple walking fearfully along the fence. People inside of the Embassy came out and invited them to come in. At the end of the discussion, people brought a ladder and the couple landed in the gardens.

Edith found the crowd frightening. People were everywhere. In the last days, more and more refugees forced themselves into the embassy and refused to leave. Edith also noticed the Czech police circling around the embassy. They made futile attempts to stop the in-rush. Two days ago, Hans-Dieter Genscher, West Germany's Foreign Minister, arrived in Prague. The veteran diplomat came to find a diplomatic solution in the interest of the refugees. He understood the refugees well; he himself had gone through similar experiences.

214

In 1952, he left East Germany for the freedoms and opportunities of the West, but he never abandoned hope that a peaceful unification of his homeland would become a reality one day. *Is that day coming now?* For the present moment, Hans-Dieter Genscher was the hope of four thousand people.

The Hotel Bishop's House is situated near the U.S. and the West German Embassy and is midway between the Prague Castle and the romantic Charles Bridge. John and Edith needed a walk after the disturbing day, and decided to have dinner in the Castle. The medieval charm of the Castle caused John to dream. It was as though making a trip in a time machine. Prague Castle is the largest ancient castle in the world. The wooden fortress surrounded by earthen bulwarks from the Ninth Century took its classical facelift nine centuries later, during the reign of Maria Theresa.

The charming walk stopped in the popular Golden Lane, where the goldsmiths lived and worked in the Seventeenth Century. John and Edith chose a small restaurant in one of the tiny colorful houses built right into the arches of the Castle walls.

"You haven't told me anything about yourself, Edith," remarked John. "How did you choose the West Berlin University for your studies?"

"My grandmother supported that idea," said Edith. "She was even enthusiastic about it. She was present at the foundation of the Berlin Free University, you know."

The world spun John around. He was lucky to be sitting otherwise he would collapse.

"Is your grandmother of Berlin origins?"

"No, she is not. She is from Ukraine. After the war, she arrived to Germany. I am proud of her, John! She was in West Berlin during the blockade, if you remember in 1948 and 1949. Now, I am here, witnessing another historic event. This is amazing! I am sure, she would be proud of me!"

"She... she..." John was not able to pronounce a word.

"Are you okay, John?" said Esther, worried.

"Yes, I am all right, thank you," said John composing himself. "Is your grandmother alive, Edith?"

"What kind a question is that! Of course, she is alive!"

"What is... what is her name, Edith? What is her maiden name?"

"Esther Kohlberg. Why do you ask? Why do you want to know?"

"I was curious," answered John. His face was white. He wanted to drink a glass of water, but his hands were shaking. Esther is alive and this beautiful young girl in front of him is her granddaughter! He wanted to jump and embrace her and ask many question about this wonderful grandmother, whom he knew well. He controlled himself though. Forty years have passed and he did not want to revive forgotten memories. Esther, perhaps, never said a word about him to her family. For a moment, he had to think about it; he needed time. He remained silent for the rest of the evening. Edith did not notice. The young student was so thrilled by the events of the trip that she was not attentive to John's silence.

When they entered the West German Embassy next morning, the disturbance was at its highest. The crowd awaited the Foreign Minister, Hans-Dieter Genscher, who had to arrive at every moment. Negotiations with the East German authorities ended. Erich Honecker had consented to a face-saving deal. On that day of September 30, 1989, Hans Dieter Genscher spoke from the balcony of the Embassy.

"Dear Fellow Citizens, I have come to you today to inform you that your journey into the Federal Republic of Germany is now imminent, your immigration is agreed. We will organize a train for your transportation. You will be able to go to West Germany, but your train must cross East German territory first."

Worried whispering and inquietude filled the air. The refugees did not trust East German authorities. Hans-Dieter Genscher held up both his hands asking for silence.

"Erich Honecker wants to claim that he had expelled you and cancelled your citizenship. We will include the refugees from Warsaw in your train. You have to be ready in the coming days!"

The crowd was relieved. The way of freedom had opened its gates. The marvel of the moment filled the hearts of those present, John and Edith among them. John decided to organize a seat on the train. As an observer, he wanted to accompany these people toward freedom. The STASI, the East German Secret Police could attempt an action against the train when it crossed East Germany. He wanted to be part of the expedition. Edith though had to fly back. He would order it. She did not have to take any risks.

John did not take into account Edith's enthusiasm. The young girl was upset. What is this? How can it be possible? Fly back to West Berlin, now, when the confrontation is coming?

"John, this is not possible! Do think about it a moment! You will be on the train, with all these refugees and you will understand nothing."

"Edith, this is simple. It could be dangerous. I am responsible for you. I do not want you to take risks. You will fly back to Berlin!"

"I do not want to fly back!" yelled Edith, determined. She crossed her arms behind her back as always, when something important was happening to her. "I want to be part of that! I want to share this experience with these people! I do not know them, but I do know the price of freedom and democracy! That is the moment of history, when we take our share by standing with them and support the ideas directing our lives! You must understand that!"

John was looking at her. He noticed the well-remembered gesture, the well-known fire in the voice; he perceived the same words; he heard the gentle singing accent; he saw the determination. The big green eyes magnetized him. He felt as though he was dreaming. He took the gentle face of Edith in his hands and gazed into these green eyes with tenderness.

"Oh, Edith! You are exactly as your grandmother."

"My grandmother? Did you know my grandmother?" asked Edith, with astonishment, and at the same moment, incredible amazement took over her spirit.

John took out his wallet. He looked for the old, yellow photo from forty years earlier. His hands were shaking, when he handed it over to Edith.

"You are the American pilot! She never spoke about you, but we all knew this photo in the family! That is amazing to see you here in front of me!"

She was laughing with her jingling voice, and embraced John as a family member. She kissed him on the cheek and smiled with her most seductive smile.

"Do you see, John? That is the reason why I will go with that train. I always wanted to be as my grandmother. I always wanted to be as courageous, as determined and without doubt as she was. I will go with you on this train and you will be happy that I will be with you."

She kissed him once again, then turned back and went to her room to prepare her luggage. John was unable to move from the lobby. He truly hoped the train would cross East Germany without difficulties.

They were at the railway station next day. The train rolled in. More than four thousand people were waiting. The railway station of Prague was full. People were also outside. Many were whispering. They could speak with loud voice, but the unusual conditions of that travel forced them to whisper. They wanted to protect a secret. Little by little, order instilled and everybody took a place in the train.

John and Edith were among the refugees. They noticed some journalists also. The passengers were tired, but determined. They left everything behind them. The majority of them did not even have luggage. Single young people, whole families, friends, lovers, young and older persons took their place in the coaches. The train departed and slowly began to roll toward freedom.

When the train came to the East German border, the more than four thousand passengers held back their breath. The train stopped. Border guards accompanied by the policemen and officers of the STASI, the East German secret police boarded the train. After having her passport inspected, Edith stepped out into the corridor. The officers were formal.

"Good, day. We are from the state security and will collect your identity cards now," they said.

The East German refugees hated the men. They represented forty years of controls, censures, and repression. With hate, they threw their identity cards on the floor at the foot of the officers.

"There is your card!"

"You cannot threaten me anymore!"

For a moment, Edith feared that the officers would answer the insult. The officers, however, bent down to collect these documents.

The train slowly rolled forward. After a few more hours, it crossed the West German border. Tension lowered; passengers were relieved. They began to cry. They are here. They arrived. They had nothing, they did not know, what tomorrow would reserve for them. At that moment, it was not important. The winds of freedom blew into the coaches through the open windows. They arrived at home.

Chapter 50
The Engagement

A long and lasting kiss united Edith and Peter. Peter had a small apartment in West Berlin not far from the Consular Section. Since he met Edith, the apartment became more comfortable. Her feminine touch softened the atmosphere of military discipline. Peter looked to Edith with tenderness. Her face was still smiling.

"Good morning, Peter!" she said.

"Good morning, Honey!" answered Peter and tightened his embrace. Edith, like a small kitty, blotted against the hairy chest of Peter. She was looking the ring on her finger.

"Oh, Peter! I am extremely happy! I love you." The events of the last days fascinated her. Sharing the importance of the historical moment with him increased the love she felt for him. Cherishing the same ideals and taking part in the same experiences amplified the strong sensual relationship they already had for each other.

The fast changing world around him motivated Peter to create an anchor point in his life, around which his world would revolve. This point would be Edith, and nobody else. Her enthusiasm, radiant nature, and always-smiling beautiful face filled the dreams of his bachelor life. Edith was happy to accept his proposal. A new life was at the beginning for the two young people.

Now that she discovered her grandmother's secret, an idea struck her, not leaving her mind in peace.

"Peter, we will organize a party to celebrate our engagement!"

"Yes, I think it is a good idea!" nodded Peter. *Oh, women always find any occasion to organize a party!* "Whom you would like to invite?"

"My grandmother and John," answered Edith.

Peter gazed to Esther with astonishment. He understood at this moment the idea. They were talking and talking about the connection between Esther and John. That was a sad story, but beautiful.

"I do not know, Edith, if it is a good idea. Perhaps, they do not want to meet. You have to be sure!"

"I will invite my grandparents and you will invite John's wife!" said Edith. By all indications, Edith already made up her mind. Nothing would stop her now.

"You have to tell them."

"Of course, I will tell them, not long before the meeting! It will be our engagement party. We will have the major role of the evening! Oh, Peter, I am excited about it!"

Peter smiled.

"When do you want to organize all this?"

"Let's see... Why not on November 9th, 1989? It will be a wonderful day!" she said laughing in her jingling style.

"You will be on your own, Edith. I am going to Leipzig with John," said Peter. He also thought he would find a favorable time to inform John about all this. He rushed to the shower, and left the apartment in a hurry. He did not want to be late. He turned his head upward, when he unlocked the car. Edith was at the window, smiling and sending kisses to him. He laughed and started the car. Happiness filled the air.

Chapter 51
In Leipzig

The taxi had difficulty in advancing in the overcrowded downtown of Leipzig. John and Peter arrived in the middle of a freedom rally demanding a democratic transformation of the East German communist regime. Every Monday in Leipzig, demonstrations took place at the Nikolai Church. They swelled into mass protests. The town of Goethe and Schiller was in high emotion. Police officers tried to contain the crowd. John and Peter were relieved when the taxi stopped at the Hotel Fürstenhof, in downtown Leipzig.

Erich Honecker and the hardliners at the head did not hear the people's protest, did not understand anything. They were ready to use weapons if necessary to preserve their power. The specter of a repetition of Tiananmen Square shaped at the horizon.

The East German communist regime celebrated their fortieth anniversary. General Secretary Mikhail Gorbachev arrived in East Berlin for the celebration. The Soviet delegation already knew that the East German regime was tottering. Outside, at the torchlight parade of Communist youth, the marchers began to chant another name: "Gorby! Gorby! Help us!"

As the leaders met at the closing reception, a plot was hatching against Erich Honecker. A group in the East German Politbüro had decided to get rid of him. Honecker was planning to stamp out the new opposition. No one was sure how far he would go.

John and Peter arrived to Leipzig, where the waves of demonstration were continuous. If Honecker went too far, he would do it here. As soon as they registered in the hotel, Peter and John walked to the Nikolai Church. The street at Nikolai Church was filled with demonstrators. That night, the police charged and scattered the demonstrators. John and Peter had difficulty in avoiding the charge of the police. The opposition groups, however, called a new gathering in two days.

Behind the neoclassical façade of Hotel Fürstenhof, John and Peter did not feel the overwhelming anxiety that permeated the city. The blond-wood armoires, green curtains and little round tables gave a Vienna-like atmosphere to the hotel room. The past glamour still existed in the old building. John and Peter feverishly called their intelligence connections to receive the latest information.

The regime mobilized paramilitary brigades, sending more than eight thousand men to Leipzig. The military received ammunition in quantities twice as much as normal. The hospitals ordered blood reserves and spare beds. What the Soviets tanks would do? They are here, in Leipzig. John was hanging on the phone.

"Do you have some inside information?" asked John the intelligence officer in Berlin, with fear in his voice.

"They will not intervene. We have assurance of that. Viacheslav Kochemasov, the Soviet Ambassador ordered the Soviet troops back to the barracks. He stopped all maneuvers and the flights of military planes. Good luck for you there!"

"Thanks," answered John. He was relieved. At least, no complication would come from the Soviets.

The city of Leipzig was in state of emergency. Shops closed at five o'clock. In the evening of October 9, 1989, seventy thousand people were already on the streets. The communist leaders begged the opposition groups to talk with them. Nobody listened. The police cordoned the entire downtown standing in a phalanx with their helmets and shields and facemasks. The crowd tightened together. John and Peter saw the crowd pushing back the East German police and troops. The agitation was at its highest. Nevertheless, the police did not open fire. The demonstration ended peacefully.

John and Peter gazed to each other. Would it be possible that this was a turning point? That feeling wide spread into the atmosphere. Events compelled the communist hardliners to implement transformation. John and Peter entered the Auerbach Keller restaurant to have a dinner and a good German beer. Goethe had the inspiration for his *Faust* in that restaurant. Old German history mingled with the impact of that historic day.

"I think we have to fly back to Berlin in a hurry," said Peter.

"I agree," answered John. "Moreover, you have your engagement party, Peter! I am happy for you. Edith is a delightful young person. You are fortunate."

"I know, John. I wanted to prepare a surprise for you. I invited Veronica. She will be there."

"Thank you, Peter! That is a surprise, but a pleasant one! I missed her and thank you for that sensitive gesture."

"That is something more, John. Edith wanted to give you another surprise."

"What is it? Why are you as mysterious?" asked John suspiciously.

"She invited her grandparents," said Peter, relieved. He did not agree with Edith to introduce the former acquaintance without warning. He was right. John's face went white. Knowing that Esther was alive brought him emotions; meeting her face to face would be a challenge. He finished the beer, nervously. He had to think about that.

"It is late, Peter, we have to go," he said abruptly changing subject. "Our job becomes increasingly mesmerizing. Don't you think also? I believe with firm conviction that the East German government will change in the coming days."

"I agree, John," answered Peter. He understood the feelings of his friend. The air of the night, filled with electricity of the day, refreshed them while they walked back to Hotel Fürstenhof.

The events followed with an incredible speed in Berlin. In the Communist Party, the allies deserted Erich Honecker. The entire Politbüro voted him out of power. His successor, Egon Krenz, promised democratic reforms. On November 1, 1989, he visited Gorbachev in Moscow. The supporter of the reforms overcame the hardliners.

The East German citizens, however, disliked Krenz. The disturbances continued. Several hundred thousands of people gathered every day at the Wall on each side. Egon Krenz offered new freedoms, in vain. His party jargon did not set well with the people. Street demonstrations grew bigger. When Veronica landed on the Tegel airport, a crowd of half a million people had gathered in East Berlin.

The engagement party would take place in the midst of historical upheaval.

Chapter 52
The Wall Comes Down

John's wife, Veronica, was elegant in the black cocktail dress. The white pearl necklace decorating the dress gave her an aristocratic appearance. She was agitated, filled with a mixture of amazement and fear. She knew what Esther had meant to John. *This is a rare and beautiful miracle of life, to meet someone intimate from our past forty years earlier; someone, who left in our soul an undeletable path. This is as a gift.* Veronica was experiencing the emotional turbulence of challenging competition. She wanted to be at her best.

She was looking into the mirror and saw John, standing in the doorstep. He was smiling. He felt the thoughts of his wife.

"You are attractive, Veronica!"

He embraced her and kissed her neck. They were standing embraced for a moment. "You do not know, how grateful I am for coming here and wanting to share this moment with me. It means much for me. Thank you for all these years of support and love."

"Oh, John, you are pathetic. I am happy to be here."

"But now, take care of me. How do I look? Am I an old man?"

"Oh, John, of course not!" Veronica laughed as she arranged his tie. "You are perfect!"

They left the hotel room and headed to the salon, where the engagement of Peter and Edith would be announced. *This will be an exceptional evening.*

Otto Fischer was in his late sixties. His biblical stature always drew attention to him. He was an active man full of energy. Today he was particularly anxious. He knew about John, however, they had never spoken in details about the journey Esther had made to arrive in Israel. He knew the KGB arrested and seriously injured her in 1949 in Eastern Germany at the end of the blockade.

The KGB did not want to hand her over to the Allied authorities. Instead of transporting her somewhere to a gulag in the Soviet Union, they put her and her uncle in a convoy heading to the newly born state of Israel. She was very sick and near to death in the transport. Her inner strength bound her to the life once again.

In the kibbutz, she took long time to heal. Otto remembered the first day she came out to work with the settlers. They were cleaning up the agricultural land from stones. Esther came slowly with uncertain steps. When she arrived to the land, she fell on her knees. She began to dig out the stones from the earth with her bare hands. She worked even though crazy with fever. She sobbed, but tears did not come to her eyes. Otto wanted to approach her. Rachel, one of the settlers stopped him.

"Let her be, Otto. She has to go through it."

After a while, her sobbing stopped. Esther was tired. She fell on her palms, and tears, relieving tears flowed on her face. Rachel and two other women stopped working and approached her at that moment. They embraced her without saying a word. Rachel helped her to get up and accompanied her to the village. Esther never cried again.

A tremendous enthusiasm lived in Esther. It was impressive. Otto took care of her, feeling that it was as a mission to give her a new direction. They found each other in the challenges of the heroic construction of Israel. They made a perfect couple united by the same ideals and sharing the same principles.

Today, Otto was pacing up and down in the hotel room, in his best suit. At first, he was upset about losing his cherished granddaughter, the daughter of his first born son, to an American military officer. He had also to face his wife's memory from the past. It was not a comfortable feeling. He tried to be practical. He could not avoid it; he would go through with it.

He looked at his wife as she slipped into her dress. Esther wore a two-piece ensemble, red as wine. She liked bright colors. *I've had enough dark period in my life, I want bright colors,* she was used to say.

She looked nice; moreover, she looked young! The Mediterranean sun darkened her face, underlining even more the special color of her hair.

"Esther, we will be late..."

"I am ready, Otto. Give me your arm... I need it for more reason than one."

Otto took her hand and kissed it.

"You have nothing to fear, my dear. You are delightful."

They left their room with rapid steps and went to the salon. Otto opened the door and they entered the room. Edith was smiling to them and wanted to make the introduction. It was not necessary. John and Esther spotted one other instantly. They made uncertain steps and met in the middle of the salon. They were still gazing into each other's eyes, not saying a word. John stretched his arms and took Esther's hands in his.

"Esther... Esther."

"John, here you are."

In the salon, a great silence reigned. The intimate moment touched everybody's hearts. They were looking without being able to say a word. The moment gave rise to feelings of sympathy, tenderness, and tearfulness. John embraced Esther and they stayed in the middle of the salon for a while. At the end, John broke the silence.

"Esther, let me introduce you to my wife, Veronica," he said.

"How do you do?" said Esther with her singing accent, which became more significant through the time. She had not spoken English in a long time. "I am glad to meet you!" Esther turned instantly toward Otto. "This is my husband, Otto Fischer. Come here, Otto!"

The atmosphere in the room relaxed. The guests began to talk and indeed, they had much to say. They had to cover forty years of history mixed with the extraordinary events of the last months. Stories of the popular unrest, claiming free travel and democratic changes, amazed Veronica. She was delighted that her husband was part of these events. Otto, from his side, felt particularly proud of his granddaughter, who found a way to participate in a democratic movement. The discussion, of course, turned to the news of the moment. Peter switched on the television. They all turned their attention to the reporter announcing the latest news.

Günter Schabowski, the leader of the East German Politbüro told journalists in Berlin that the restrictions on travel to the West would be lifted.

The guests of the party stared to each other. Is it true? Did that mean the gates would open? They heard rushing steps in the corridors. They took their coats and hurried to the streets as many other guests of the hotel. The streets were full with people, all sprinting toward the checkpoints.

The border guards were puzzled. They had not received instructions. They tried to get in touch with their superiors, but nobody responded to them. The armed guards had one single order: *stop anyone trying to escape.* The crowd from each side of the checkpoints exerted a tremendous pressure on the guard. All of a sudden, they gave in — and opened the barriers.

Edith and Peter heard people bellowing ahead of them. Esther and John began to applaud. Otto and Veronica stayed frozen by amazement. Through the open gate, Germans from East Berlin began to pour into the arms of Germans from West Berlin. Edith and Peter were running among the people.

John and Esther were in the middle of the crowd. The overall excitement took over their feelings. They knew they were taking part in a historic event once again. The world was changing its look. The purpose of all that they lived forty years ago took shape today. This was the ultimate reason for what they fought so many years ago! Freedom, democracy, civil rights and progress.

Esther and John never did see the Wall; they had left the city before its construction. Nevertheless, their lives were part of that Wall. The tyrannies symbolized by that Wall destroyed their love. Holding each other's hand, they were contemplating Peter and Edith.

This was same place, same lovers, same story, but what a different outcome!

John and Esther were staring to each other. West Berliners began to demolish the Wall in front of the Brandenburg Gate. John and Esther knew at this moment, their sacrifices had been essential and necessary. They had to wait forty years to understand their destiny. The world entered in a new era and they were artisans of this new world.